About the Author

Jennifer Shand lives in central Virginia with her husband. After graduating from James Madison University and working with children for many years, she began to write for them. She is now the author of several books for children, from the very young up to teenagers. Jennifer loves to write, travel and to spend time with her husband and family. She also enjoys photography, being outside, hiking and reading.

The Last Elf Daughter

Jennifer Shand

The Last Elf Daughter

Olympia Publishers
London

www.olympiapublishers.com
OLYMPIA PAPERBACK EDITION

Copyright © Jennifer Shand 2024

The right of Jennifer Shand to be identified as author of
this work has been asserted in accordance with sections 77 and 78 of
the Copyright, Designs and Patents Act 1988.

All Rights Reserved

No reproduction, copy or transmission of this publication
may be made without written permission.
No paragraph of this publication may be reproduced,
copied or transmitted save with the written permission of the publisher,
or in accordance with the provisions
of the Copyright Act 1956 (as amended).

Any person who commits any unauthorized act in relation to
this publication may be liable to criminal
prosecution and civil claims for damage.

A CIP catalogue record for this title is
available from the British Library.

ISBN: 978-1-80439-381-9

This is a work of fiction.
Names, characters, places and incidents originate from the writer's
imagination. Any resemblance to actual persons, living or dead, is
purely coincidental.

First Published in 2024

Olympia Publishers
Tallis House
2 Tallis Street
London
EC4Y 0AB

Printed in Great Britain

Dedication

I dedicate this book to my husband, my mom and my sister – three people who are always there for me.

CHAPTER 1

IT BEGINS & FIRST LOOK

Evie kept checking the clock as she paced the living room floor.

"Mom, come on, I don't want to be late! You know the coach said we won't have a chance of making the team if we're behind schedule. Ugh, you don't need make-up to take me to soccer tryouts!"

"Oh, come on, Evie. You know one day you'll like wearing make-up too."

"No, I wouldn't count on it," Evie replied. "Seems like a big waste of time. Now, come on, let's go!"

In the car, Evie started to chill out some. "I think we're going to make it. Barely, but I should be on time."

"Oh, I wouldn't worry about it, honey," her mom replied. "You'll definitely make the team. Not only are you a great player but never forget, you are special."

Evie rolled her eyes. Her mom was always telling her she was special. "Yeah okay, mom, I'm special. Sure. I think I'm as ordinary as a thirteen-year-old gets."

Evie's mom just laughed awkwardly.

"Do you want me to go with you and watch?" her mother asked as they pulled into the parking lot for the soccer field.

"No way! I can do this on my own. I'm not a baby, mom."

Evie stepped onto the soccer field. The smell of freshly mowed grass filled the air which almost made Evie sneeze. After a few warm-up exercises, the coach split the girls into two teams and had them play a mock game changing the positions of certain players as they went. Evie stayed on offense the whole time which is exactly where she preferred to be.

Evie did great at her tryouts. She made the team, like she did every year. Usually this made her feel very happy but now it just felt ordinary. She wanted something to make things feel special, but instead it was on to the next ordinary thing. She and her mom met her dad for dinner. They did this every week. Then she ordered her favorite dinner that she ate all the time.

Evie's parents were chatting and catching up on each other's days when Evie's dad turned his attention to his daughter just as the food had arrived.

"So, how was your day?" her dad asked. "How did soccer tryouts go?"

"They went fine," Evie replied as she took a bite of her dinner. The cheese was so warm, gooey and perfectly melted. The smell of basil and oregano filled her nostrils. "I made the team."

"Well, that's great! Why don't you sound more excited?"

"No, I am excited. I mean I'm really glad I made the team. But I usually do, so it's nothing out of the ordinary."

"Yes, that's true, but you should still be excited. Don't take it for granted that you get to play your favorite sport," her dad told her.

"I know, I know. No lecture needed," Evie said as she took another bite.

"Hey, no attitude," her mom jumped in.

"And no lecture is coming," her dad added. "So, don't worry. What else is new?"

Evie's parents were waiting for a reply from her, but she just sat there staring straight ahead with a funny look on her face.

"Evie? What's up? You okay?" her mom asked.

"I don't know. I don't feel so right," Evie could barely say.

"What's wrong? What are you feeling?" her dad asked.

"I feel weird. I feel light-headed and nauseous. My stomach feels sick. I think I'll be okay. I just need to sit here for a minute."

"Do you want to eat a little more?" her mom asked trying to think of something to help.

"No, I can't even think about eating right now." Evie was scared but she didn't want to say it. She didn't know what was happening but she knew it wasn't good.

"What can we do?" Her dad was getting concerned. He could see the worry on her face.

"Nothing," Evie replied. "Just let me chill here for a second." She put her head down on the table. It wasn't helping. The nausea was getting worse and worse by the second. She felt like she was in real trouble. She just wanted to be left alone. Getting out of the restaurant was all she wanted but she couldn't yet move.

"We'll get the check and get out of here," her mom said. "We need to get you home."

"I think I need to…" Evie stood up to leave but it was too late. She couldn't hold it in and she suddenly vomited all over the table and floor. She tried to sit down but she passed out and fell to the floor.

"Evie? Evie?" was the last thing she heard.

Hours later, unbeknownst to Evie, she finally came to. She wasn't comfortable. The hospital bed was unfamiliar and every time she moved, something tugged on her. Ouch. There was something pierced into her arm. She tried to look down to see what it was and realized she was still incredibly nauseous. The sterile smell of the room and the incredibly bright and harsh lighting wasn't helping either.

"Don't try to do anything, honey," her mom said.

Evie tried to reply but couldn't get any words out. Just then the doctor walked into the room anyway. He looked concerned.

"Mr. and Mrs. Baker," the doctor started.

"Yes, please call us Noah and Rose," Rose said.

"Okay, could I speak to you in the hallway for a second," he said with a glance at Evie. Evie would have been more curious why he didn't want to talk in front of her but she felt too sick to care right now.

Evie could see the doctor talking with her parents. Everyone looked worried but she couldn't hear what they were saying. A nurse opened the door and walked in and as she did, Evie heard a sliver of the conversation.

"…it appears she was poisoned…" the doctor was saying.

The door closed and Evie could no longer hear anything. She did see her mom's face change to confusion though and she could read her mom's lips say, "What?"

Noah and Rose came back into the room and attended to their daughter.

"What was that about?" Evie managed to ask. "What am I doing here?"

"You got sick at dinner, sweetie. You, uh… got a bad case of food poisoning," Rose answered with a nervous glance at Noah. "But everything is fine, so don't worry."

"So, it was just food poisoning. Like normal food poisoning?"

"Yes, of course," her mom answered while shifting awkwardly.

Evie tried to sit up and tugged on her IV again.

"Whoa, honey, don't try to get up yet. We don't need you to

start projectile vomiting again," her dad said trying to make her smile.

Evie cracked a small smile. "I feel so sick. And I have a huge headache."

"We'll ask the doctor for some medicine for your headache," Rose replied. "But I think they've given you as much anti-nausea medication as they can."

"I'm never eating at that place again," Evie grumbled. "And I don't think I'll ever be able to eat lasagna again. That's a bummer. I love lasagna. Or at least I used to. When can I go home? I don't want to stay here."

"Well, sorry my dear, but the doctor said you have to stay here for at least tonight," her dad said. "Maybe longer."

"That's a bummer too," Evie said as she closed her eyes. It was getting late but she also wanted to sleep to avoid the discomfort of the pain and nausea.

Evie's mother watched over her as she slept. They looked so much alike. She was tall and slender like her mom and just as beautiful.

The next day, Evie felt a little better and she was ready to leave the hospital. Her parents knew they weren't leaving the hospital just yet though. They kept hovering over her and being slightly annoying.

Evie thought that her parents were acting weird. She was getting a vibe that didn't match up with what they were telling her. "What's going on?" she finally asked them. "Why do you keep staring at me?"

"Well, you're in the hospital," her mom replied as she looked sideways at her husband.

"Can we get out of here now?" Evie asked. "I just want to go home."

"Sorry, but the doctor wants to keep you overnight again," Noah reluctantly told her.

"What? Are you serious? I have to sleep here again? Ugh! It feels like I've been here forever. Why do I need to stay again?"

"Trust me, we're not thrilled to be here either," Noah said. "But we have to do what the doctor thinks is best."

Evie just rolled her eyes.

"Don't worry, we'll get you home in time for school on Monday, sweetie" Rose said to her daughter. "Hopefully, you'll feel up to going. I would hate for you to miss your first day of eighth grade."

"I wouldn't hate it," Evie said with a small smile.

"Oh, come on, you love school," her dad said.

"Love? Really, dad?" Evie replied.

"Okay, okay, but you like school, right?" Noah asked.

"School's okay, I guess," Evie said.

"Well, either way, I would hate for you to miss your first day," Rose said. "But let's not worry about that now. I just want you to rest."

The nurse came in with more medication. It made Evie very sleepy. She was dozing in an afternoon nap. As she was sleeping and coming in and out, she overheard her parents talking. She wondered if she was hallucinating because she swore she heard them saying some crazy things. But being half asleep, she only caught bits and pieces.

"...can't believe my brother thinks this was someone trying to kill..." Rose said. "What if Cy's right?"

"Honey, let's not get carried away..." Noah said trying to keep everything calm. "We don't know..."

"...Cy does make sense..." Rose continued. "Someone may want to kill Evie... I think... we told her the truth. Put an end to both of our secrets…"

"There's no reason to tell…" Noah replied. "Especially before we know anything for sure."

"Noah, she needs to know now…" Rose said. "It'll be easier to keep her safe if she knows."

"…just an accident," Noah said. "It's too early to tell her."

Evie wanted to wake up and listen better but she just couldn't. She was too out of it. She fell into a deep sleep and the conversation seemed like a dream. Once she woke up, she had forgotten about it completely.

She spent the rest of the day being seriously bored in the hospital room. It went by slowly.

The next morning, it was finally time to leave the hospital. Evie woke up feeling much better and got up and out of the hospital bed.

"Hey, are you sure you feel up to that?" her mom asked. "We can get you a wheelchair."

"No way, I don't need a wheelchair," Evie answered. "I'm good".

"So, you're feeling up, chuck? Noah said with a funny smile on his face.

"What?" Evie said slightly confused. "Stop being weird, dad."

"Oh, come on! Upchuck? That's funny! Get it? Upchuck? It's another word for puking. You do know that, right?" He asked Evie as she just looked confused. "Wow, we have really failed the next generation," he said to Rose.

Evie's parents were happy to get her out of the hospital but not as happy as she was to leave.

"I can't wait to get home," Evie said in the car. "I'm looking forward to showering and sleeping in my own bed tonight."

"Oh, I bet," Rose said.

"We'll be there soon," Noah added.

"Yeah," Evie replied. "I usually love living in the country but this curvy road is making me feel sick again. I always thought our house was in the perfect spot because it's far enough out to be so quiet but still close to the city. But now I wish we were closer to the hospital."

Evie lived in central Virginia with an incredible view of the Blue Ridge Mountains, which lived up to their name with several shades of delightful blues. The mountains provided beauty and a sense of safety.

When Evie got home, she took a quick shower and then immediately started texting her best friends, on a group text.

Finally got out of the hospital, she wrote. *So happy to be home. Just got my schedule today. Did u get ur class schedule?*

Evie's phone chimed back right away. It was Kat. *Awesome u r home! Yeah, I got mine. First class is History. Homeroom with Nimes. Yuck! He's the worst. Feeling better?*

Evie texted back, *Oh that sucks! My first class is History too! Yay! Homeroom with Garland. She's not too bad, I guess. Yeah, feeling better, sort of.*

Her other friend, Rion, who was also her cousin, texted back too. *Bout time u got out of there. Ur such a drama queen. Got my schedule. Homeroom with Nimes too so great.*

Oh good, I won't have to deal with Nimes on my own. Kat wrote.

At least u two will have homeroom together. What's ur first class? Evie replied.

Yeah, cool. History. Rion replied.

Awesome! We all have first period together.

Cool! Kat replied.

Yeah, that's cool. Rion replied.

That's if I make it to school at all. Maybe I can use being sick to miss the first day. Evie texted.

Again, such a drama queen. Rion replied.

You better come to school! Don't leave us on the first day. Kat replied.

The first day of school came quickly and Evie really didn't want to go. She told herself that she didn't feel all the way better but deep down she knew she just didn't want to go because school was so boring. She tried to use her illness to get out of going but it didn't work. Her mom and dad weren't buying it.

In first period, the teacher was taking roll. "Eve Baker," the teacher called. "Yes, that's me," Evie replied, "but everyone calls me Evie."

"Okay," said the teacher as she wrote down Evie on her sheet.

Evie's best friend Katherine smiled at her. She knew her name would be called next. They had been together alphabetically in classes since elementary school. That and the fact that they had both always been tall for their age had bonded the two girls since they were little and they had been best friends since first grade.

"Katherine Barton," the teacher called next. "Here," Katherine replied as she raised her hand and widened her already big brown eyes, "but everyone calls me Kat." When Kat and Evie were younger, Kat had been invited to a slumber party that Evie had not been invited to. Kat didn't go and instead invited Evie over to her house to stay the night. Kat thought that Evie didn't know about the other party but Evie did and this really solidified their friendship. Kat was also a good listener which was good because Evie liked to talk. Kat was kind but she would stick up for herself if need be, especially on the soccer field where an aggression came out of her that existed nowhere else.

"All right," the teacher said, "anyone else have a different name for me to call them?" Evie's cousin raised his hand and the teacher said, "Seriously? Well, what's your name?"

"It'll be listed as Orion Wilton, but please just call me Rion," Rion said as he brushed his light brown hair from his eyes. Some people in the class giggled, mostly girls who thought Rion was cute.

"I can't believe dad gave me a name I would always have to tell people to shorten, just like him," Rion whispered to Evie and Kat. "He knows how annoying it is."

"I thought your dad's name was Cy," Kat whispered back.

"Yeah, it is, but that's short for Cygnus," Rion whispered back to her.

Rion was slender like his cousin and they both had beautiful blue eyes but with different shades. Rion's were a deep sky blue and Evie's were more icy blue. Rion and Evie had grown up together because his dad and Evie's mom were brother and sister and super close. They had spent so much time together that Rion was the closest thing to a sibling that Evie had and vice versa. Rion was a good person but he did like to pull pranks. Once there was a kid who was being a jerk to him, so Rion managed to swipe the kid's backpack and fill it with silly string. Evie and Kat found this hilarious.

"Okay," said the teacher, "is that all? Anyone else with a different or shortened name?" She wrote down these two extra notes about Kat and Rion and one other student. After that, no one else raised their hand, so she just continued with the roll call.

Right after this, the teacher had them breaking into small groups to work on questions that she had handed out. Evie, Kat and Rion quickly formed their group.

"So, you made it here today, after all? Didn't convince your parents you needed to stay home?" Kat asked Evie.

"No. They just kept telling me I could do it and I didn't feel like arguing, so here I am," Evie replied.

"I can't believe you were in the hospital for a couple of days," Kat said. "I had food poisoning once and oh my gosh, it was terrible, but I didn't even go to the hospital. You must've had it bad! How're you feeling?"

"Oh, I feel better now, but it was terrible when it happened. I was eating and all of a sudden, I felt so sick," Evie replied. "I threw up all over the place. It was embarrassing."

Kat and Rion started laughing. Evie couldn't help but to laugh too.

"Sorry," Kat said. "We shouldn't laugh, that's not funny."

"No, it's okay," Evie said. "It is kinda funny. But it was also crazy. It was like I blacked out or something. Throwing up is the last thing I remember until I woke up in the hospital."

"Wow, that is crazy," Kat said.

"Yeah," Evie replied. "I couldn't believe how bad I felt. I felt like I was going to die."

"I thought you were dying the way dad was acting," Rion said. "He was all in a panic and saying we had to get to the hospital and something about getting the guy. I was like, 'who, the cook?'" Rion said laughing. "But seriously, he was really worried and it seemed like something else was going on. Like something more than just food poisoning. Dad was really upset and frustrated. He seemed like he was in disbelief that this happened. I was like, 'it's just food poisoning,' but he was like, 'why is this happening'?"

That reminded Evie of the conversation her parents were

having that she partly overheard when she was half out of it in the hospital. She was thinking of this which gave her a surge of anxiety and she must've looked a bit distant because Kat was suddenly like, "Evie, are you okay? You still with us there, girl?"

"Oh, yeah," Evie answered. "Well, actually, I don't know. Rion reminded me of something." Evie continued to kind of stare off into space as she tried to remember.

"Well, what is it?" Kat asked as she leaned in and tucked her brown hair behind her ear.

"I'm trying to remember. When I was sleeping in the hospital, I thought I overheard my parents saying something weird. I just figured I was really out of it or dreaming because it sounded so out there. But now I am starting to wonder if maybe there's something more going on here. Maybe I really did hear them saying these crazy things."

"What did they say?" Rion asked.

"I'm not completely sure because I was half asleep, but I think they said that someone like…" Evie lowered her voice as much as she could and continued, "…tried to kill me. Too crazy, right? That can't be what they were saying."

"Yeah, that can't be what they were saying. That would be insane," Kat said. "I don't think you heard them right. But was there anything else?"

"Well, I also thought I heard them talking about Uncle Cy and I guess they told him something since he was acting weird. But your dad didn't tell you anything, Rion?" Evie asked looking at her cousin.

"Nope, he just said that you were in the hospital and it seemed like you had food poisoning. But like I said, the way he was acting didn't match up with that."

Evie looked confused. "But this is if I can even trust you,

Rion. Are you just pulling a prank on me? Like you have a hundred times in our lives? Is this like the time you tricked me into eating an acorn because it was 'just like a peanut' or when you convinced me to wash it down with vinegar?"

"No, I promise, Evie," Rion said looking serious. "I am telling you the truth. Dad was acting all strange. I swear this is not a prank."

"Because I have always forgiven you for all your pranks. I'm a very forgiving person. But this is serious."

"I know. I wouldn't mess with you about this," Rion replied. "Dad really was acting strange."

"Yeah, my parents were acting kinda weird too. And they were talking about how and when to tell me… the truth. But what that 'the truth' is, I don't know. Whatever it was, it seemed like it was a big deal."

"That is weird. Maybe you were dreaming," Kat said.

"Yeah, maybe," Evie replied while trying to think back. "I had to be dreaming."

"I don't know," Rion disagreed. "It seems very strange that I heard something and you did too. And like I said, dad was acting weird. More than weird, he was almost panicked. Now that I think of it, I heard dad, when he was talking to your mom, saying, 'you should definitely tell her'. That matches up perfectly with what you thought you heard."

"Tell me what, I wonder," Evie said.

"I think you should ask Uncle Noah and Aunt Rose about it," Rion replied.

"But I'll seem crazy if I ask that! I guess I could blame it on all the meds!" Evie replied with a small laugh. "Besides, what am I supposed to say? 'Hey mom and dad, was that food poisoning or did someone try to kill me?' I mean, really! And even if it's true, do you think that they'll tell me? From what I could make out, they didn't agree on whether to tell me or not."

"Only one way to find out," Rion replied and even Kat nodded in agreement.

"This may seem crazy, but I think there are too many coincidences to ignore it," Kat added.

"Okay, I guess I will," Evie said. She did want to know and even though it would be awkward, she really wanted to ask her parents and clear this up. What if there was something going on? She had a right to know. As she was thinking on this, she noticed a new kid who was looking at her. He had blonde hair and was kind of tall like her. She didn't know his name, but she thought he was very cute and suddenly she forgot everything about asking her parents. Now all she could think about was this new cute boy who was staring at her.

CHAPTER 2

FIRST TRUTH & SECOND TRUTH

Evie was both apprehensive and eager to talk to her parents about what she overheard in the hospital. The apprehension made her wait until the weekend to bring it up. She was also preoccupied with thoughts of the new boy whom she shared two classes with and many looks at each other throughout the week.

But when Saturday morning came, she couldn't wait any longer to find out what was going on. She felt excited and nervous about what she may find out. Maybe, she thought, her parents would not tell her anything or maybe there was nothing to tell. On the other hand though, what if there was something to tell? She wondered if she could handle it if there was something truthful about what she thought she overheard. She kept thinking to herself, *there's nothing to be scared of. It's probably nothing. And they're your parents. They always say you can talk to them about anything. Just go for it. It'll be fine.* So, finally, she just went for it.

"Hey, Mom, Dad, can I talk to you about something?" she started.

"Of course, honey, what's going on?" her dad answered as her mom looked anxious.

"Well, it'll sound crazy, but when I was in the hospital I thought I heard you guys saying something... something about someone... that someone... um... tried to kill me." She was about to say, "I know, that's crazy, right," but the looks on their faces made her stop. "Is this crazy or what is going on?" she continued, starting to feel a little worried.

"Well, you're not crazy—" her mother started, and Noah interjected.

"No, Rose, we are not ready to do this."

"Yes, we have to do this; for her safety. Please, Noah?" Rose asked. Now Evie was feeling even more nervous.

Noah saw the look on Evie's face and realized she was nervous. He didn't want her to be left wondering and worrying about this so he decided it would be best to just tell her the truth. "Okay. I guess we can't put it off any longer," Noah agreed.

"Well, where do we start," Rose said with a distant look in her eyes.

"Just start!" Evie snapped, as this was freaking her out.

"Okay, sorry sweetie," her mother replied with a concerned look. "I'm just going to start at the beginning with something we have held off on telling you for a long time," Rose's heart swelled with happiness. "Evie, you know how I am always telling you, you are special. Well, I am not just saying this. It is true."

"Of course you think that, you're my mom," Evie said as she grew impatient.

"No, Evie, this isn't just a mom thinking her child is special. You are actually different," Noah said trying to help Rose.

Evie was about to say something when her mom just cut in.

"Evie, you are an elf."

Evie didn't know what to say and she just stared at her mom for a moment, so Rose continued.

"I know, you are thinking, that I am just making this up, but I'm not. I promise you sweetie, this is real. You are an elf."

Evie continued to just stare at her parents. She didn't know what to say.

Her mom started talking again, "Maybe you're wondering, what is an elf. Well, we are just like humans, really. But we're a more ancient people and we have a special kinship with nature. We are usually tall and in the past, there were some elves that had magical powers. Nothing too crazy, just slight magic and they would mostly act as doctors for their people. But there hasn't been an elf with magical powers for some time now. Most elves do have extreme senses though. We can see further than humans and we can hear things from further away."

Evie's head was spinning. "An elf?" she muttered. "What are you talking about? What does that even mean? I'm an elf? I thought that was a made-up thing. Does that even really exist?"

"Yes, being an elf is a real thing and you are one," Rose said.

"Oh, you're messing with me, aren't you?" Evie asked slightly laughing, but from their faces she knew they weren't messing with her. "This is crazy! This can't be real! An elf? Like Santa's elves?" Her mind was spinning so much that she had forgot that someone may be trying to kill her.

"I know, I know. It's a lot to take in. But yes, elves really do exist. And no, not the Santa Claus version of tiny elves that make toys or anything. More like the elves from *The Lord of the Rings* and *The Hobbit*. Isn't that cool? You love those movies." Rose paused here.

"You're really not kidding here, are you?" Evie asked. "This is for real?"

"Yes, this is for real. But don't freak out. Being an elf is not weird. Like I said, we're just like humans mostly. All this means is that..." her mother briefly paused, "that you are special. But things do not have to change. Well, actually they may have to change. Because of the poisoning..." her mother whispered mostly to herself. "Oh, there are so many things to tell you. Okay, so your life should pretty much stay the same. An elf is not that different from a human and you're still a normal kid who will have friends and go to school. But you are special because..." her mother struggled on this a little, "because you are the last known female elf in America that could still continue the elf people."

"The last female elf in America?" Evie wondered aloud.

"Well, the last one that we know of and that could still have children one day," her mother added. "There are other female elves but they're all older, like me."

"So, you guys are elves too then?" Evie asked.

"Yes, I am," Rose answered.

"But no, I'm not," her dad replied. "But because Rose is, you are one."

"I still need to explain that to you," Rose added.

"This is all too much." Evie was seriously confused. "Okay... this all sounds crazy. And I don't really know what to think about it, but it doesn't sound like it changes my life very much. Right?" Evie said, wondering why her parents looked so concerned.

"Well, that's true," her father tried to help, "but now there is more to the story; something that was just recently added. You may be in some danger."

"Oh," Evie said as she started to remember the whole someone trying to kill her part.

"Let me go back even further," her mother said. "As I said, elves are an ancient people and for tens of thousands of years, we just kept to ourselves. Since we look just like humans, humans didn't even know we existed. We just blended in. We never married humans and so elves were just with other elves and everything was fine. Of course, there were some elves that would fall in love with humans, but it was forbidden. That is, until the marriage of King Arthur to Guinevere, an elf."

"What?" Evie interjected. "King Arthur is a real story? And Guinevere was an elf?"

"Yes and yes," her mother replied. "King Arthur was a real king and Guinevere was an elf. Merlin was an elf too. He was the most magical elf that ever lived. That is how King Arthur met Merlin. The elves introduced them. But that is another story, back to King Arthur and Guinevere. They randomly met one day and there was an instant attraction between them. It did not take too long and they fell in love. Both of their parents were against them being together at first but the two of them became inseparable. Then Guinevere's family started to wonder if it would be a good thing for elves to enter royalty and they also wanted their daughter to be happy and Arthur made her happy. Arthur just defied his father at first, but eventually his father gave in too because it was hard to tell Arthur what to do. When they got married, everything changed. It was a famous wedding among humans and elves but for different reasons. It was famous among humans because Guinevere wasn't royalty and Arthur had fallen in love with a commoner. It was famous among elves, because it was the first time an elf married a human. As I said, it was allowed because the elves thought this could be a good thing for them to enter royalty. But mostly, it just opened the door for change. And after that, elves started marrying humans. Then for many years, this was fine and no one seemed to care. The elves only told their spouses that they were elves and it didn't really spread much, so most humans still didn't know of elves. Then, over time, elves started to realize that not all children from elves and humans were elves. It took some time to figure it out but eventually they realized that if a male elf married a female human, the children were not elves. But if a female elf married a male human, then the children were elves. So, they realized that a male elf can't have elf children and only female elves were able to have elf children. Only female elves carry the gene that can be passed down to make a child an elf."

"This is confusing," Evie said.

"I know, sorry about that. But to explain it further, females have two X chromosomes and some traits, such as being an elf, are X-linked which means they are only found on the X chromosome and are then passed on by the mother. So, only female elves can pass on the elf gene. To put it simply, only a female elf can have elf children and continue the people. That is where you come in," Rose looked at Evie.

"What do you mean?" Evie asked.

"Well, like I said, since only female elves can create an elf and you are the last one we know about that could still have children one day, then it is kind of up to you to continue the elf people in America."

"Oh man," said Evie, still not knowing really what to think. "That's a lot of pressure."

"No! That is exactly what I don't want you to feel. Look, Evie, I don't want you to think that it's up to you to continue an entire people," her dad interjected. "You are just a kid and you do not need to think about this. You need to focus on school and soccer and just being a normal thirteen-year-old girl."

"Then, why are you telling me this?" Evie asked. "You could've just lied to me."

"See, that's what I wanted to do," Noah said.

"I was kidding, dad," Evie said. "I'm glad you told me. I think."

"For the record, I wanted to wait to tell you until you were older," Noah said. "I think this is too much pressure for a young mind to comprehend and too big of a secret for a kid to keep."

"I'm not a little kid anymore," Evie said rolling her eyes. "I can keep a secret."

"Good, because this needs to be kept secret," Noah added.

"Okay, okay," Evie grumbled. "What's with the mood?"

"Well," Rose continued with a stern look at both Evie and Noah, "I have always wanted to tell you. It's a special thing we share together, that we are both elves. But we are telling you now because unfortunately, there is still more to this. The reason I felt you needed to know this now is that you may be in danger."

"Yeah, so back to my original question that someone was trying to kill me?" Evie remembered. As she said this, fear swelled inside of her.

"Yes, back to that," her mom replied as she took in a deep breath. "First, let me say that we're not even sure that you are in danger. But you may be, so we need to tell you everything so we can keep you safe. We are worried that someone may want to end the elf people and so it would make sense that this person would go after you because if you are no longer around, then no one can have elf children anymore."

"What about you, Mom?" Evie asked.

"That's sweet of you, honey, but we don't think I'm in danger. I'm pretty much too old so this person probably thinks that I'm not having any more kids, which is correct."

"Why do you think that I'm in danger?" Evie asked. "Did something happen?"

Rose looked to Noah and he took the reins on this answer.

"You know the food poisoning you were just in the hospital with?"

Evie nodded and said, "Yeah, what about it?"

"Well, the doctor told us that you were poisoned. Not by food, but with actual poison. He said it appeared that someone intentionally poisoned you."

"Just wait a minute." Evie's head was spinning and she finally realized that she needed to sit down. They all went and sat down at the dining room table.

"Okay, tell me about who might be… trying to kill me," Evie struggled to get the words out.

"We don't really know anything about this person," Noah continued. "We initially thought it must be an accident or some kind of mistake and I still think it may just be an accident, but after your mom told your uncle about it, he was the one who thought this was someone trying to kill you to end the elf people. Your mom thinks he is right, but I'm still not sure."

"Why does Uncle Cy think that?" Evie asked.

"It was really the only reason we could think of that someone would poison you," Rose added. "I mean, why else would someone try to kill you? And there have been a few instances of it in the past; from a very long time ago, some female elves were killed by people trying to end the elves all together."

"But this is crazy, why would someone, who doesn't even know me, want to kill me? I haven't done anything bad to anyone. I'm innocent."

"Yes, you are," Noah said. "But this isn't about that. This is just because of what you are, not who you are. It's a terrible thing, but unfortunately some people are targeted because of what they are all the time. It's blind hatred."

"What do you mean, 'blind hatred,'" Evie asked.

"Well, it's complicated but the point is it can lead to someone hating another person when they don't even know that person,"

Noah answered. "I can't even understand when a person hates another person that they don't even know."

"Yeah, I don't understand that either," Evie said.

"We really don't know the motives of this person, the poisoner," Rose said. "It may be hatred of elves for some reason or it may be something completely different. Your uncle didn't have a theory on why this person wants to end the elf people and we don't either."

"So, wait, are Uncle Cy and Rion elves too?" Evie asked.

"Uncle Cy is an elf too because our mom, your grandma, is an elf," Rose answered. "But no, Rion's not an elf because his mom was not an elf."

"Is that why Uncle Cy and Rion's mom got divorced when Rion was little? Because Uncle Cy was an elf?" Evie asked.

"Oh no," Rose answered. "There were many reasons, sweetie. But I'm sure it wasn't because of that."

"Does Rion know about his dad being an elf?" Evie asked.

"No, Rion doesn't know yet," Rose said. "Cy has kept it from him for us, because we knew Rion would tell you. And Cy wanted to tell him so bad. That was a big favor he did for us."

"Well, at least I don't have to be mad at Rion for keeping this from me," which was all Evie could think to say. She just kind of sat there staring for a minute trying to take everything in. Suddenly more questions hit her.

"Is grandpa an elf?" Evie asked her mom.

"No, just my mom is," Rose answered.

"I guess your parents aren't elves, dad, since you're not one," Evie said looking at her dad.

"No, they're not," Noah answered. "Actually, they don't even know about the whole elf thing."

"They don't? Why?" Evie asked.

"Well, I've just never told them. It's such a shocking thing for someone to learn and even sort of unbelievable. Now I'm glad I didn't tell them because I don't want them to know about the danger, either. They would worry so much and there's nothing they can do, really."

"Well, I get that," Evie said. "It is a shocking thing to learn. I just don't know what to think. I feel like the same person, but I also feel like I'm different or something. Like I'm weird or something. Does that make any sense?"

"It does," Rose said. "I know exactly how you feel. But believe me, you are the same person. You're still the same wonderful girl you have always been. There is nothing wrong with you or strange about you."

"Yeah, Evie, I didn't mean that I haven't told my parents because I think you are weird or something," Noah said. "I don't want to make you feel like you won't be accepted because of it. There is absolutely nothing wrong with being an elf."

Evie nodded her head, but she still wasn't sure how she felt about it. She just sat there not knowing what to say.

"I know this is a lot," Rose said. "Do you want me to stop or keep telling you more?"

"Keep telling me more?" Evie almost shouted. "Are you kidding me? There's more to tell?"

"Well, just where we are now with this and where we go from here," Rose answered. "For the most part, we want you to go about life as if you didn't know. Just keep living your life as you did before. We want you to live as normal of a life as possible. But there will be differences now. You have to be extra careful and of course, be wary of strangers or people that seem out of place."

"Yeah, duh," said Evie.

"Hey now, be nice," Noah said. "But there will also be changes to how we treat you. We will be keeping a closer eye on you and you won't be able to just go anywhere or do anything. You will need a chaperone when going out."

"Wait, what? A chaperone?" Evie asked, not liking this part of the conversation at all. "Like everywhere I go? I don't think so. I'm not going to lose my independence. I don't need people constantly watching over me."

"Yes, you do," her father said. "Look, Evie, we knew you wouldn't like this, but it is not up for debate. We have to take this very seriously. You could be killed. This is as serious as it gets."

"But you said you're not even sure about Uncle Cy's theory, dad. What if Cy's wrong? I may not even be in danger."

"We can't take any chances," Noah answered. "It's true that there is so much we don't know but we do know that you were poisoned so that is significant."

"But you also said you wanted me to live as normal a life as possible," Evie said. "That will make my life very un-normal. This will make me miserable."

"Oh, don't be dramatic. We will try to keep it to where you barely notice it," Noah continued. "But this is as normal as possible. Having a chaperone is the 'as possible' part of that. We promise to hang back and keep our distance. We'll be at soccer practices too now instead of just games and if you go to the movies or something with friends, we will just sit somewhere else away from you."

"No way!" Evie said. "I don't want my parents hanging around watching me like I'm a little kid. That would be so embarrassing! I am not going along with this!"

"Well, you have to," her mother said. "I'm sorry, but you don't have a choice."

"I guess I just won't go anywhere now," Evie said, completely frustrated. "So much for it not changing my life very much. It sounds to me like it's changing my life completely. I don't want any of this! How could you guys have not told me that I was an elf? Now, instead of finding out this good news for the first time, I am finding out all this bad news that goes with it! You should've told me I was an elf way before this!"

"Please don't be mad, Evie," her father pleaded. "We thought we were doing the right thing." With this, he got a look from Rose. "Well, I thought I was doing the right thing. Your mother wanted to tell you. I just wanted you to be a normal kid for as long as possible. I thought this was a lot to put on you and a ton of pressure and I didn't want you to feel that pressure. I wanted you to focus on school and just have friends and have fun. I was trying to protect you."

"Well, I get that," Evie said. "I'm glad that you let me be a normal kid for as long as possible. But now I know and things aren't normal anymore. I don't even know what to think right now."

"Yes, we know this is so much to take in. Just take your time to digest it," Rose said trying to console her daughter.

"Yeah, right now, I'm done," Evie said as she walked away towards her room.

Rose and Noah looked at each other with their own frustration but they couldn't help but to understand. "That's fine," her mother said. "I know you have a lot to think about. But please don't be upset with us, Evie. We are only doing this to protect you. We just want you to be safe."

"Let us know if you need anything or if you have any questions," Noah shouted to add.

Noah waited an hour before checking on Evie. He just

wanted to make sure she was okay. "Hey honey, everything okay in there?" he asked through Evie's door.

"Yes, I'm fine, I just want to be alone," Evie answered.

"Okay. You're not going to run away to live in a tree and make cookies, are you?" Noah said trying to lighten the mood and make Evie laugh.

"Haha, Dad," Evie replied. "This isn't a commercial. I'm not a Keebler elf."

Noah couldn't see Evie so he didn't know that he did make her smile.

CHAPTER 3

THE ASSIGNMENT & NEW FRIEND

As Evie lay on her bed in her room, her mind was in over drive about being an elf. She must have thought about texting Kat and Rion a hundred times and started to several times but never did. This just wasn't something you could put in a text. And for a thirteen-year-old girl, that is saying something. She wanted to see them in person but she also needed time to herself. So, telling them would have to wait for now. She stayed in her room all day just thinking about everything her parents had told her. Though she didn't fully understand how scary the situation really was, she was scared. Of course, she was thinking about this mysterious person who was trying to kill her, but surprisingly, she was mostly thinking about being an elf. She felt like this was a really cool thing and she liked the idea of it. It made her feel special. But she was also thinking about how she was the only one who could carry on the elf gene. It felt like a ton of pressure. Not that she was going to be having kids any time soon. It was all just weighing on her and by evening, she was starting to go crazy. She finally came out of her room and went downstairs to the living room.

"Hey honey, how're you feeling?" her dad asked.

"I don't know," Evie answered. "I still don't know what to think. I really don't want to think about it all anymore. Could I have a friend over or something?"

"Actually," her mother answered, "Cy and Rion are coming over for dinner. We told Cy that we told you and he was so happy about it. He is dying to see you now. He told Rion everything too. That should be a good friend to talk to right now, huh?"

"Yeah," Evie replied but she couldn't decide who she wanted to talk to or if she even wanted to talk. She just knew she wanted some company instead of being in her own head for any longer.

Evie's uncle Cy busted in the door when he got there and immediately gave Evie a big hug.

"I am so happy you know now!" Cy exclaimed. "No more secrets for all of us," he said as he looked around at all of them. "But now we can also talk about how best to protect you, Evie. It will take everyone and we all should be vigilant. Everyone needs to keep their eyes open and look for anything suspicious. This person could be anyone. It may be someone we know, but it may not."

"Okay," Evie's dad said. "Let's not overwhelm her again. She already stayed in her room all day. I'm just glad she's out here with us again."

"I was just saying that this is on *all* of us now to keep Evie safe," Cy continued.

"Yes, that's true," Noah said. "We'll all be vigilant. Evie will be with one of us all of the time now."

Evie rolled her eyes at this and let out a sarcastic, "Great."

"Oh, come on, what's that about?" Cy asked. "We promise we won't cramp your style too much," he said with a smile.

"'Cramp my style?'" Evie asked. "What does that mean?"

"It means you will barely notice we're even there when we're watching over you," Cy added. "We know you don't want to have a chaperone all the time, but that's just the way it is now. The most important thing is that we keep you safe."

"Yeah, we're all here for you, Evie," Rion added. "Just let me know if you need me or if anything is scary for you or if you want someone to go places with you. You can count on me."

"Well, you're not old enough to be a chaperone, Rion," Cy said. "But nice try."

"Thanks though, Rion," Evie said. "It is nice to know that I have all my family for this." Though Cy and Rion were trying to make her feel better, she was starting to feel more scared the more they talked. It was starting to feel more real that she was really in danger. "I don't really want to talk about it anymore."

"Well, I do," Rion said. "Evie, you're an elf! I didn't even believe dad at first. I was like, 'sure Dad, whatever you say. By the way, have you been drinking?'"

This made Evie laugh, which was exactly what she needed.

Rion continued, "I mean an elf? Does that really even exist? But it's so cool."

"Yeah, I guess it is cool," Evie replied. Now talking to Rion was making her feel better.

"It just leaves me wondering," Rion said in a serious tone, "Evie, what is Santa really like?"

"Oh, ha ha," Evie said as she playfully pushed Rion.

"No, I really want to know," Rion replied. "And when you go to the North Pole, do you take a plane or do the reindeer come and pick you up?"

"You're such a nerd," Evie said but she couldn't help but laugh.

"This really is cool," Rion said. "Because now, I mean I was going to ask for a new bike for Christmas but now you can just make me one."

"I think that's enough, Rion," Cy said. But Evie was enjoying the distraction even if it was at her expense.

"Oh, come on, I have a bunch of these," Rion said.

"Well, who's ready to eat?" Rose asked as she made her way to the dining room table with the pasta. "Cygnus, can you grab the garlic bread and bring it in here for me?" she asked her brother.

"Of course, but you know I don't like to be called by my full name," he replied.

"Sorry, I just forget sometimes," Rose said.

"Then, why did you name me Orion and not just Rion?" Rion asked his dad.

"Yeah, I just wanted to keep the constellation theme going," Cy answered. "My bad."

During dinner, the conversation kept going back to protecting Evie, which was making Evie upset. She just wanted to talk about something else. Rion noticed her face and he sensed she wanted a new subject, so he interrupted.

"I almost forgot," Rion said. "I'm not sure if you even know this or not, Evie, but does Gandalf wear anything under that robe?"

After this, the conversation carried on without talking about protecting Evie and she was glad for it. The rest of the night was the distraction that she needed.

Monday morning came slowly. Evie had texted Kat to come to school early so she could tell her something. Kat couldn't wait to get there to hear what Evie had to say. Thankfully, when Evie finally saw her best friend they had an empty classroom, so she just blurted everything out, telling Kat everything her parents had told her. She spoke as fast as she could because she knew she didn't have much time before class started. At first, Kat didn't believe what Evie was telling her. Evie though, didn't pause long enough to let Kat ask any questions. By the end of it, Kat could tell by how serious Evie was that she was telling the truth.

"You're an elf?" Kat asked when she finally had a chance to talk. "I was not expecting that! I mean, I was very curious about what you were going to tell me, but I would never have guessed this. And so, it is true that someone is trying to kill you? That can't be! What are you going to do? Is it safe to keep going to school?"

"I'm not sure what is and isn't safe now," Evie replied. "Mom is going to be driving me to school every day now and she will probably be at soccer practice too. I will definitely be losing any independence that I had. Between mom, dad and Uncle Cy, I will have someone with me all the time when I'm not at school."

"Well, that kinda sucks. I guess we won't be going to do much then, huh?" Kat replied.

"Yeah, it really sucks," Evie replied. "I'm not happy about it at all. But I still want to do stuff. I don't want this to change things. I'm determined to still be me. They said they will keep their distance, so maybe it won't be so bad. And maybe they will all calm down eventually. They just need some time, you know?"

"I hope so," Kat said, wanting to not feel like she was going to lose her best friend. "But someone being after you is pretty serious, so I don't see them letting this go any time soon. I don't see how this won't change things. But keeping you safe is super important obviously, so I guess it's all for the best."

Just then, people started walking in including Rion, as first period was about to start. "Did you tell her?" Rion asked Evie, nodding towards Kat.

"Yeah, everything," Evie said.

"You probably already know, but you can't tell anyone, any of this," Evie said to Kat.

"I promise," Kat said and Evie knew she could trust her

friend.

"Okay, everyone," the teacher started, "we are going to start a project that will be twenty percent of your grade, so take it very seriously. I need everyone to pair off. You and your partner will be picking a president from two choices that I will give you and putting together a presentation for the class."

Evie, Kat and Rion immediately all looked at each other. Splitting into pairs? Now what?

"Well, who should pair with who…" Evie was starting to say, when the cute new boy walked up to her.

"Hi," he said.

"Hi," said Evie.

"Do you have a partner for the project?" he asked.

"Uh…" Evie didn't know what to say.

"No, she doesn't," Kat said.

"Do you wanna be my partner?" the cute boy asked. "My name is Logan."

"Shhure," said Evie still kind of stunned. Kat nudged her with her arm and Evie came to a little more. "I mean, yeah, that would be great. I'm Evie."

"Yeah, I know," Logan said.

With Evie and Logan pairing off, this left Rion and Kat as partners, who didn't mind since they both secretly had crushes on each other.

The rest of the day, all Evie could think about was Logan and the fact that they were now partners and would be working together on this assignment. There was just one problem. Logan had invited her over to his house to work on the project that weekend and Evie was sure this was not going to go over well with her parents. Normally, this would have been fine, but with this new issue of someone trying to kill her, Evie wasn't normal.

And the last thing Evie wanted was one of her parents or her uncle hanging out at Logan's house with her.

Now that the ice had been broken between the two, Evie and Logan talked more during their classes together and they were becoming friends as the week progressed. They discovered they were the same age and it was crazy how well they got along. They liked the same music, TV shows and movies. It was also a plus that Logan was a fan of *The Lord of the Rings* and *The Hobbit*, yet Evie kept why to herself. It was not taking much time at all and they were getting very close. Logan was still expecting Evie to come over on Saturday to work on their project together, so Evie knew she would have to ask her parents.

When she got home from school on Wednesday, she got her parents together in the kitchen to ask them. "Okay," she said, "First, I need you to understand that this is very important to me. And it's not just important to me, it's important to my grades. I have this project to do for History class and it's twenty percent of my grade and I have a partner to work with on it and his name is Logan and he is new at school and we really need time to work on this and he is really nice and he invited me over to his house this Saturday to work on the project together and I really, really want to go." She finally took a breath and looked up at her parents.

Her parents could see that this was important to her and they both couldn't help but notice the smile that came across her face when she said Logan's name. "Well," her father started, "why can't, what's his name, Logan, come over here instead? That would make us feel better about your safety."

"Because, ugh," Evie was already frustrated, "Logan already invited me to his house and I don't want to seem like some weirdo that can't go to other people's houses or something. I mean, what's the big deal? If one of you drives me and I go straight in and stay there the whole time and then one of you picks me up, then everything will be fine, right?"

"I'm not sure," her father said. "I mean, we don't even know his family."

"Yeah, Evie, I get this is a big deal for you," Rose said. "But like we said, you are special and we have to treat you a little differently."

"I don't want to be special! And you also said you wanted me to have a normal life," Evie said, using that against them again. "What if I promise to stay there and go straight from your car to the house and back to the car again? Then can I please go?"

Rose and Noah looked at each other and decided to give in to their daughter. "Yeah, I guess so," her father said after looking at her mother again for confirmation. "But we have to meet his parents first."

"Ohhhh, do you have to? I don't want to ask him that," Evie whined.

"Yes, sorry sweetie," her mother replied. "That is a definite. We have to meet Logan and his parents."

"Logan too?" Evie exclaimed.

"Well, of course," Rose continued. "What are we going to do, go over there and ignore Logan? Trust us honey, this is normal, this is what people do and it will not be weird at all. I'm sure he will introduce you to his parents too."

"Well, yeah, I guess so," Evie said but she still didn't like this.

So, on Saturday afternoon Rose and Noah drove Evie over to Logan's for her first real outing since the revelation. Evie had made plans with Logan for them to come over and as embarrassing as it was, she made plans for her parents to meet his parents. It wasn't so bad, since Logan said his parents wanted to meet her parents too. Maybe Noah and Rose were right, and this was normal and not as weird as Evie thought it was.

It turned out that it was actually pretty normal. Evie and her parents went inside and Noah and Rose introduced themselves to Logan's parents, Max and Claire. They were happy to meet each other and Rose and Noah were glad to meet Logan and Max and Claire were very pleased to meet Evie.

"So, how long have you lived here?" Rose asked. "Evie mentioned that Logan was new at school."

"Yes, we moved here over the summer," Claire answered. "It seems like such a nice area. Max got a new job here, so that's what brought us here. He's teaching at the university. The boys were not too happy about moving, but Logan has already seemed happier about it," she said as she looked at Evie.

"So, boys?" Rose asked. "Does Logan have a brother?"

"Yes," Claire answered. "He's around here somewhere. His name is Carter. He's older than Logan. I don't know if we'll see him," Claire said as she looked around. "I think he's having a harder time adjusting to the move but he'll get there."

"Oh, yeah, I'm sure he will. It will get better for him," Rose said.

"Well, we hope you like the area. It's a great place to live," Noah added.

"Yes, we already really like it," Max replied. "The mountains are beautiful."

"Yes, they are, we love them too," Rose said. "Well, we better let the kids get to work on their project. It is twenty percent of their grade." Max and Claire cordially agreed and Rose and

Noah left feeling a little uneasy about leaving their daughter with people they barely knew but they knew the kids would not leave the house and they would be there to pick her up in a couple of hours.

Evie and Logan went to the den to work on their project. After an awkward double "hi" and "how are you" with both responding "good," Logan said, "Well, I guess we better start with picking our president. Um, we have the choice of John Adams or Grover Cleveland. Let's look them both up and see which one we like best."

"Sounds good," said Evie. "I like the name, Grover. That's a funny first name. Isn't that a Muppet?"

"Yeah, I think it is," Logan said with a small laugh.

"The Muppets are funny," Evie said and then regretted it instantly, hoping it didn't make her sound like a little kid.

"Yeah, they're hilarious," Logan said which made Evie feel relief.

Logan sat down on a chair with a laptop and Evie stood behind him so she could see the screen too. She noticed that she liked the way his hair looked from the back.

"Well, one interesting thing about Grover Cleveland is that he is the only president, so far, who served two terms but they weren't back to back. He was the twenty-second and the twenty-fourth president," Logan said.

"That's kind of neat," Evie replied. "I like it that there's something different about him. Anything different like that about Adams?"

"Let's see," Logan was looking as Evie looked over his shoulder. She was leaning in to see better when he glanced back and she suddenly became aware of how close she was to him so she took a step back. She worried that she had crowded Logan.

"Oh, sorry," Evie said.

"No need to be sorry," Logan replied. "You're totally fine. Okay, so Adams was the first president to live in the White House."

"Well, that's cool too," Evie said. "But I think I like the one where he was president twice but not in a row. And I don't really know much about that president, Grover, what was it, Cleveland," she said as she leaned in closer to Logan to look at their assignment. "Besides, I like his name too."

"Yeah, me too," Logan replied as he looked at her face up close. He got distracted for a second by how pretty she was, but came to and said, "That sounds good to me. Grover Cleveland it is. I guess we can get to work."

Just then, someone suddenly came into the room and startled Evie. "Hey, loser, whatcha doing? Oh and you have a friend here. Well, who is this?"

"Hey Carter, this is my friend, Evie. We have a project to work on for history class so can you please leave us alone," Logan replied as he knew Carter would try to embarrass him.

"Sorry," said Carter. "Well since my little brother has no manners, let me introduce myself," he said as he turned to Evie, "I'm Carter, Logan's older brother."

"Nice to meet you," Evie said. She noticed that Carter had very dark hair and didn't look much like Logan.

"Well, nice to meet you too. So, tell me about yourself, Evie. What are you in to? What are your hobbies, goals and dreams?" Carter was trying to bug the two of them but Evie being a little naïve thought he was being sincere.

"Oh, uh, I play soccer," Evie started to say but Logan interjected.

"You don't have to answer him," Logan said. "He's just

being a jerk."

"Now that is hurtful," Carter said to his brother. "I was really interested in your little friend. I'm sorry, Evie, obviously Logan's in a bad mood or something."

"I'm not in a bad mood. I just want you to leave us alone," Logan replied.

"So testy," Carter said. "Evie, you seem like a normal person, what are you doing hanging around this weirdo?"

"Carter, will you please get out," Logan almost yelled.

"I guess I will leave you two alone so you can work on your project, as long as that's all that is going on. I fear you have changed since you started getting arm pit hair," Carter said as he made a face at Logan trying to embarrass him.

"Oh my gosh, just get out," Logan stood up and yelled.

"Okay, okay," said Carter as he left the room.

"Sorry about that," Logan said to Evie.

"Oh, that's fine, it was nice to meet your brother," Evie replied.

"Yeah, I guess. He's not always nice. Well, at least not lately. He used to be pretty cool, but…well, I don't know what's up with him."

"How old is your brother?" Evie asked.

"He just turned eighteen," Logan answered. "Anyway, let's forget about him and get back to work."

As Logan and Evie worked on their project, they talked and laughed and had a really good time together. The time flew by and before she knew it, Evie's parents were there to pick her up. That night, Evie and Logan both went to sleep thinking about the other.

CHAPTER 4

THE WIND & NEW SKILLS

It was Evie's favorite time of year. Not only did she love fall because the leaves were changing but she loved the air. Living in an area where the air in the summer was thick and sticky with moisture, the air in the fall was perfectly crisp and dry. She loved the smell of falling leaves and it made her feel like the air smelled clean. This time of year was fun too because she was starting her new soccer season and she was pumped to play. Kat was also on the team which made it even better. They went to practice every day together. It was so great having her best friend there with her. And Kat knowing Evie's secret about being an elf and being in danger was especially helpful. Kat understood why Evie had a family member there every time to watch every practice in its entirety. Some of the other players picked on Evie for this. She tried her best to ignore it, but it did bother her. She didn't want to seem like a spoiled kid who was over watched by her parents or that she was being babied by her family.

The taunting would have been worse, but for some reason, Evie was playing great this year and so her teammates only gave her but so much grief because they wanted her to keep playing. She had always been a good player, but she felt like something had changed. It was like she knew which way the ball was going to go and exactly how the ball was going to soar through the air. She couldn't make sense of it but she felt like she could see the air or the wind and which way it was blowing. She loved feeling the wind glide across her face and she knew everything about it. She knew its direction, she knew its speed and she knew what type it was. She could feel slight variations in the temperature of the wind. It was like she had a kinship with the wind and a sixth sense about it. Even beyond that, it felt like her mind was connected to the wind and could kind of control or manipulate it. Evie thought it was crazy to think this and so she just kept playing without talking about it. But she did keep playing great and she knew something was different. It was like she could predict everything the ball was going to do.

In her first game, things were not going so great for either team. The game was almost over and the score was zero to zero. It had been a grueling game. Both sides had been trying so hard to score and were giving it all they had. All of the players were exhausted and disheartened. Evie felt like she had never ran so much in her life and yet she still hadn't had a good chance to get up to the goal. There wasn't much time left on the clock and she knew she had to make a drive towards the goal. She finally had her chance. A player on the other team kicked the ball to another player on their team and as the ball was flying through the air, Evie could see that the ball was going to arc a little closer to her than the kicker had intended. With this chance, Evie jumped up and intercepted the ball with her chest. She was close to the goal and started charging towards it. It was a little blustery and the wind was different today. She knew she could use the wind to her advantage. As she reached the goal, she kicked the ball into the wind. She could somehow see the wind and although it looked like she was kicking the ball straight, the wind carried the ball on a small curve, just as Evie knew it would. The goalie was not expecting the small curve and the ball went soaring past her outstretched arms and right into the net. The whole team ran over and jumped on Evie. When she finally emerged from the team's embrace, she found Kat and hugged her and they jumped up and down.

"How did you get the ball to curve like that?" Kat asked. "That was crazy. It was like it had a mind of its own."

"Not exactly," said Evie. "I think I knew it was going to do it. It was like I could see the…"

Just when Evie was about to say she could see the wind, her coach interrupted them and said there was still a minute left to play. Just a little later and Evie's team was celebrating their first win. Everyone was rallying around Evie and high fiving her. She felt great and was mostly just enjoying this win and the excitement around it. Part of her though could not help but to keep wondering how she pulled off the game winning score. She knew it sounded crazy, but she knew she could see the air and exactly how the wind was blowing. She wanted to stay and celebrate with her teammates but she also wanted to talk to someone about this new development. The team hung out for a little longer to celebrate but soon they started breaking up and heading home. Unfortunately, Evie never had a chance to talk to Kat alone to share this new development. Evie got in the car with her mom and dad, who were also congratulating her and celebrating.

"Wow, what a first game! What a great ending! I did not see that coming. I thought the game was going to end zero to zero, since there was only like a minute left," her dad said when they were on their way home. "How psyched are you, sweetie?"

"Oh, super psyched," said Evie, but her mom immediately noticed that she sounded distant.

"What's wrong, honey?" her mom asked. "You just won

your first game and you scored the winning goal but you sound upset."

"Nah, I'm not upset," Evie said. "I just have something on my mind." Evie paused but decided she had to talk to someone about this and her parents just might be the best people for it. "I don't really know how to explain this, but there was something different about me when I was playing tonight. Ugh, how do I explain it? I feel like I'm always sounding crazy with you guys lately with the things that I bring up."

"You will never sound crazy to us, just say whatever it is you need to say," her mom said trying to comfort her.

"Well, lately, when I have been playing soccer and other times too, I feel like… like I can see the… the air or something. It's like I can see the wind and I can feel what it is going to do or that I could change it if I wanted to. So, now you can tell me I'm crazy and that that's impossible. But I'm telling you, I could see the wind when I scored the winning goal tonight. I could see exactly how the ball was going to travel and which way it was going to go and…"

"Slow down, honey," her mom said with a huge smile on her face. "This isn't crazy at all! In fact, it's super exciting! Seeing the wind is an elf trait! Remember when I told you that we have a special kinship with nature? Well, this is part of that connection. It's an ability that not all elves have, like me, I don't have it, but it's definitely from you being an elf. Your uncle Cy though, he can see the wind and manipulate it too. He is going to be so excited to hear that you have the trait too. It used to be very common among elves but there have been fewer and fewer who have had the trait and Cy was starting to worry that the trait was ending. Cy is going to want to work with you and teach you how to use it."

"How to use it?" Evie asked feeling confused on how she could use it beyond soccer.

"Yes, how to use it," her mom continued. "As you already discovered, you can use it in soccer but there are other ways to use it too. I will wait and let your uncle tell you about more ways to use it. He can teach you how to alter it too. You and he will have to get together this weekend."

"Okay," said Evie. "That sounds like it could potentially be pretty cool. But I feel like you're keeping something from me."

"I just don't know how to explain all the ways you can use the wind," her mom said as she fidgeted with her hands. "Trust me, you'll be better off waiting for your uncle to describe everything."

"Okay, not cool. But I guess I'll have to wait," Evie said and then she looked distracted again. "There's just one more thing bothering me. Do you think it's cheating to use this to score in soccer?"

"No, not at all!" her mom and her dad both said.

"Did you actually change the wind when the ball was in the air?" her mom asked.

"No, I wouldn't even know how to do that. I know I said I felt like I could, but I wouldn't be sure how to. I could just see the direction of the wind and how it would naturally carry the ball on its own and I kicked the ball into the wind in a certain way."

"Then no, I don't feel like that's cheating," her mom said.

Her dad added, "Using this is just like using any other trait a person may have that makes them good at sports. It's just like being a fast runner or being good with your foot work. It's just another trait that makes you a good player."

"Thanks for saying that, Dad. That makes me feel better," Evie said.

"Just don't actually change the wind once you learn how to do that," Rose said.

"Yeah, I get that," Evie said.

She rode the rest of the way home feeling pretty good about things. This was a great night. Not only did she find out that she could see the wind and would be carrying on an elf trait that was really cool, she was going to be better at soccer and winning tonight felt so good. Of course, she also felt pretty good that she saw Logan in the stands watching her game.

Evie's mom called her uncle Cy immediately when they got home the night of the soccer game. Evie listened as Rose told him about her seeing the wind. As predicted, Cy was so excited and thrilled to find out Evie was carrying on the trait. He was ready and eager to teach Evie more about this skill. They were going to meet Saturday evening at Evie's house. Evie wasn't nervous about it, as she thought it would mostly be like a glorified soccer practice. She couldn't even think of what he might be teaching her other than more ways to be better at soccer. *What more could you do with seeing the wind*, she thought.

When Saturday evening came, she was surprised when Cy wanted them to leave the house right when he got there.

"We need some elevation and the roof is too high," he said.

"What are you talking about, Uncle Cy?" Evie asked as she was thoroughly confused.

"I haven't told her about what you will be doing," Rose told Cy.

"You haven't? Why not?" Cy asked.

"I didn't want her to be nervous and over thinking it. I was scared she would back out or something," Rose said.

"Back out of what? I hate being kept in the dark! What are you guys talking about?" Evie was getting a little concerned and annoyed.

"Well, honey, today your uncle Cy is going to teach you a new ability some elves have because they can see the wind. Some elves that can see and manipulate the wind, like you, can use this to... sort of fly."

"What? Fly!" Evie exclaimed. "No, I can't do that. There is no way that I can fly. I just started seeing the wind. I'm not sure I can even see it all the time. How am I going to use it to fly? What if I suddenly can't see it or something? Will I fall?"

"Now you can see why I didn't tell her," Rose said to Cy. "I was worried you would freak out a little, Evie. But please, don't worry. You will start out with jumping off things that are not too high. That is why we waited until evening, so it will be a little dark so people hopefully won't see you guys. You're going to go to the park and start with jumping off some of the play equipment. And just to clarify, what you will be doing is not technically flying. You will not be able to lift up off the ground on your own. What we are hoping for and what other elves can do is they can jump off high places and use the wind to glide safely down to the ground. They can jump out of trees and off buildings and stuff like that. So, I guess it would be better to say that you will be learning to glide."

"Why do I need to know how to do that?" Evie asked. "I mean I guess it could be kinda cool to jump out of a tree or off a building. Sounds fun, but it doesn't sound like something you or dad would let me do. Especially, since it doesn't seem necessary."

"Well, yes, this isn't something, under normal circumstances, that your dad and I would let you do, but it could be helpful..." Rose trailed off and looked to Cy, not knowing what to say.

"Trust us, Evie," Cy added. "This is important to learn,

especially for you. And it may be necessary. As we have told you, you are in danger. Someone is out there who may try to hurt you and we need to do everything we can to protect you and to prepare you to protect yourself. This could be something that could save your life one day."

"Oh, wow," said Evie. "I didn't think of that. Okay, I'm in. Let's do this, Uncle Cy."

Cy and Evie found a playground that was completely empty, which wasn't too hard, since it was a little dark now.

"Now this can be really hard to learn so don't get discouraged," Cy said. "As you said, you may not even be able to see the wind all the time, but eventually, as you practice and as your skill increases, you will see the wind all the time. Then you will have to learn how to ride the wind to fly or glide as I prefer to call it. Later on, we will practice how to change or manipulate the wind, as it may be necessary to change it, to ride it to a specific point, but it will be much later before we practice that as that is much more difficult."

"So, what do I do to start?" Evie asked.

"Climb to the middle of that ladder on that play equipment and turn towards me," Cy said as Evie did what he said. "Now close your eyes and just listen. Can you hear the wind?"

"It's barely blowing tonight," Evie said. "Maybe tonight isn't a good night for this."

"No, it's perfect," Cy responded. "It's best to learn when the wind is light and when it will be the hardest to see it. Now, can you hear it? Clear your mind and really focus. Imagine what the wind will sound like. Try to determine which direction it is blowing."

Evie focused and cleared her mind of other things and tried to hear the wind. It felt like forever, but she thought she finally heard it.

"There it is," she said. "I hear it and I feel it. It's blowing across my face from the left to the right. It's so light."

"That's right!" Cy exclaimed. "Wow, Evie that was fast. I thought that was going to take the whole first lesson. Now as you hear the wind, focus on nothing else and open your eyes as you picture it and look for it right where you hear it."

Evie opened her eyes as she was listening to the wind and looked for it. She could immediately see it. She was surprised that hearing it first really helped her see it. It was so cool seeing the wind. It was like having a sixth sense.

"I see it," Evie told Cy. "This is so neat. I love it."

"Great, Evie," Cy responded. "Now, can you see the wind and how it is traveling and how it could carry you towards the ground? I know you are not very high up, but try to imagine riding the wind towards the ground. When you jump, you jump into the wind and as you said, it is traveling from left to right, so you follow it from left to right."

"Okay," said Evie. She closed her eyes again for a few seconds to listen once more. As she opened her eyes, she saw the wind and jumped into it. She hit the ground with a thud.

"Could you feel the wind? Did it carry you at all?" Cy asked.

"I don't know," said Evie. "I could see it and I thought I jumped right into it but I also feel like I hit the ground right away without any help from the wind. I think I need to be higher up."

"Well, maybe just a little higher. I don't want to do anything too drastic," Cy responded.

So, Evie tried jumping from just a little higher and the same thing happened. She just went straight to the ground without feeling any help.

"I need to go way higher," Evie said.

"I don't think you're ready yet," Cy said with concern. "Maybe that's enough for tonight."

"No way, Uncle Cy. Please just trust me. I know I can do this if I'm up higher."

"Okay," said Cy. "But if you get hurt, your mom is going to kill me."

"I won't get hurt. I'll be careful," Evie said as she climbed on top of the monkey bars.

Evie closed her eyes again and opened them quickly as she heard the wind and knew she could already see it. She could see it traveling and knew what direction it was going, how fast it was going and how it would carry her. She just knew it in her heart that she could do this. She jumped from the monkey bars and hit the ground fast and with a thud and then sort of rolled. Her uncle ran over to her.

"Evie, are you okay?" Cy asked frantically.

"Yes, I'm fine," Evie said, but she was disappointed. "Man, I really thought I was going to do it that time. I was totally ready for it. I'm not sure what went wrong. I need to try it one more time."

"I'm not sure," Cy said. "Maybe that's enough for tonight. As I said, you've already done more than I planned for."

"Just one more try," Evie replied. "Please, Uncle Cy, I know I can do this."

"Well, okay, just one more time. But if you don't do it this time, we are calling it a night. And please be careful!" Cy said.

Evie climbed to the top of the monkey bars again. Once again, she closed her eyes and heard the wind and then opened her eyes to see it. Then she had an idea. This time, instead of jumping, she sort of fell into the wind and she glided slowly down to the ground.

"Yes!" she exclaimed. "I did it! I felt it! That was amazing! I could do that from way higher, I just know it. Where can we go to do that from higher?"

"Whoa, slow down," Cy said. "You need to do that at least twenty more times from that height then we will move on to the roof or something."

"TWENTY more times?" Evie asked.

"Yes, Evie, twenty more times," Cy answered. "At least."

So, Evie did just that. She jumped from the top of the monkey bars twenty more times and rode the wind every time. She even managed to ride it to about ten feet away. She could go further but she knew she wasn't high enough.

"I can't believe how far you came in just one night," Cy said. "I thought this was going to be weeks of practice before you were here."

"Thanks," Evie said. "Can I jump or actually, fall into the wind off the roof at home?"

"Fall into the wind?" Cy asked.

"Yeah, I feel like if I jump then I don't ride the wind but if I just sort of fall into the wind, then I glide with it."

"That's awesome. Use whatever works for you. I can't believe you found something that works already," Cy replied.

"So, does that mean I can fall off the roof at home?" Evie asked again.

"Well, I wouldn't phrase it that way to your parents, but I think you can do it. It will be up to your parents though, so we'll see," Cy responded.

Just then they both heard someone say, "Evie?" Evie turned around to see a guy standing there. It took a second but then she recognized that it was Logan's brother, Carter. "Hey, I thought that was you," Carter said.

"Hey Carter, how're you?" Evie was a little nervous Carter would ask what she was doing at the park when it was almost night, but then she realized that he was there too, so hopefully it wasn't that weird. She hoped that he hadn't seen her falling off the monkey bars.

"I'm good, just out for a walk," Carter replied.

"Yeah, us too," Evie said, "this is my uncle Cy."

"Hi there," Cy said.

"Hey," Carter said.

"Carter is the older brother of my partner for my History project at school," Evie explained to Cy. "I met him the other day."

"Yeah, Logan was really happy after you guys worked on your project that day," Carter said to Evie. "I think he really likes you."

Evie didn't know quite what to say and she was sure this made her face turn red, especially in front of her uncle. She wondered what Carter meant by "likes you." She wanted to say that she liked Logan too but she felt embarrassed in front of Cy. Hearing this did make her very happy though. "Yeah, Logan's really nice," she finally said.

"Well, we better get home before it gets too late," Cy said. "It was nice to meet you, Carter."

"Yeah, you too," Carter said. "I'm sure I'll see you around, Evie."

"See ya," Evie replied.

As Carter walked away, Cy and Evie got into Cy's car to head back to Evie's house. When they got back to the house and after some debate since Evie's father did not want her to jump off the roof, they all finally agreed to let Evie fall off the roof. Evie ended her exciting night by easily gliding off the roof of her home and floating down safely to the ground with her uncle and her parents so proud of her. Evie absolutely loved riding the wind. She loved the feeling of the wind on her face. The best part was the sensation of the wind all around her, safely surrounding her like a bubble or a cocoon. She knew it wasn't flying, but it felt like she was flying. It was so freeing. It gave her a sense of liberty and independence she was sorely lacking lately. It left her feeling happy and enthused. As exciting as all this was though, she was just as happy about Carter telling her that Logan liked her.

CHAPTER 5

THE CHASE & NEXT MOVE

For two weeks, Evie worked with her uncle Cy on learning to "fly" and Cy even started teaching Evie how to change the wind, which was much harder than her first lessons. She was getting a little better at it though, but it was going to take way longer to learn than just seeing the wind and using it to glide which came so naturally. During this time, Evie was also working with Logan on her History project. They had met two more times and were learning everything they could about the president, Grover Cleveland and putting together a presentation about him. Evie and Logan were also getting closer and becoming good friends. Logan was a lot of fun and they had similar sense of humors. They had discovered they both liked going to the movies and especially seeing comedies and action hero flicks. They planned on going to the movies together soon which made Evie very happy except for the thought of her parents sitting in the row behind them.

    The following Friday night, Evie and Kat had a soccer game on their home field. One of Evie's favorite new things was looking up into the stands at her soccer games and seeing if Logan was there to watch. So far, he was every time. The game was a good one even though they lost. Evie scored a goal and Kat did great on defense but they were pretty evenly matched with the other team and the other team barely outscored them. The score had been one to one almost the whole second half and both teams were exhausted. At the very end of the game, the opposing team managed to score another goal while Kat was the goalie and this made her very upset. She left the field feeling devastated and Evie did not feel so great either, but not as bad as Kat. They and the rest of the team were walking up to the school to get changed and commiserating about their loss and Evie was trying to cheer Kat up when Evie saw Logan was waiting at the door to the school for her. Evie's parents had made it clear that she was to stay with the other players the whole time and not be alone at any time for any reason and to come straight to the car after changing. But at the moment, Evie wanted to talk to Logan so bad. He looked so cute standing there. She had many thoughts all at once to justify it to herself. *I'm sure it'll be okay. I'll just talk for a minute. Nothing bad will happen. Mom and Dad are just being overprotective anyway.*

Kat saw Logan too and looked at Evie to see if she was going to stay with her to keep encouraging her and trying to make her feel better or if she was going to desert the team and stay with Logan. Evie stopped at the door with Logan and told Kat she would catch up with her and the team in a minute. Kat let out a huge sigh and rolled her eyes but Evie didn't think much of it. At the least, she didn't think it was directed towards her.

"Sorry 'bout the game," Logan said to Evie as the rest of the team walked into the school. "I thought you guys were going to end up in a tie. How's Kat?"

"She's pretty upset. She hates losing bad enough, but being that she was goalie for the last goal, she is not happy with herself. I tried to tell her that this happens to everyone who is goalie and to just let it go. I mean, we can't win every game. I mean, I guess we could, it's like possible but it's just unlikely. Ahh, I'm rambling. It just sucks. I hate losing. But we played a really good game and that makes me feel better, I just wish it would make Kat feel better. I know her and she is going to be bummed for a few days. She's really hard on herself with stuff like this."

"Sorry to hear that," Logan replied. "I wish she would feel better too. She played a really good game. And you did too."

"Thanks," said Evie. "I will tell her you said that. Maybe it'll help to hear it from someone who was watching the game from the stands."

Evie and Logan talked for a few minutes until Evie suddenly remembered that she was way behind on getting changed and that most of her team would be finishing up by now. She thought of her parents and knew they were going to be very upset with her for not staying with the group.

"Oh, I better get going," she suddenly blurted to Logan. "My parents will freak out if I am too late to meet up with them," she said with an eye roll geared towards her parents.

"Oh, okay," Logan replied. "Sorry to make you late."

"Oh, no it's fine," Evie replied as she didn't want to make Logan feel bad. "It was really cool of you to come to my game. It was great talking too; I just wish I had more time. I will see you at school, right?"

"Yeah, definitely," Logan replied. "See you then."

They both kind of lingered for a second just looking at each other. Evie liked the way his hair fell across his forehead. Then Evie took off quickly walking towards the locker room trying to make up some time so she wouldn't get in trouble. She may have just lost a game, but she was feeling really happy right about now. She felt like she was light as air. She was all in thought about Logan and how cute he looked talking to her and sitting up in the stands when she realized that there was a hooded figure ahead of her in the hallway. He was standing between her and the locker rooms. She slowed her walking to an almost stop. Her mind started racing. Was this just some student who was hanging out in the hallways? He looked too tall to be a student. Was it a parent waiting for their child? Should she just keep walking towards the locker room and walk past him? For anyone else, you might just shrug it off and walk right past them, but for Evie, who has someone out to kill her, she had to take this seriously. So, she turned around and started walking the other way. Just then, the hooded figure started walking after her and following her. She panicked and started to run. The hooded figure started to run after her! It was him! The person who tried to kill her before was here and out to get her again! She wanted to find a way out of the school. She tried a door closest to her. It was locked! She screamed, "Help!" and then she ran some more.

The guy was gaining on her. She then found another door. It was unlocked! She ran outside and screamed, "Help!" again. No one was around. *What should I do?* she wondered. She realized she was at the back of the school. She had to get to the front. She started to run around the side of the building, when she saw a staircase that led to the roof of the building. He was almost right behind her and there was no doubt that he was going to catch her before she reached the front of the building. She had to think of something quickly. Suddenly, she decided to climb to the top of the building. He followed her up the stairs and was still gaining on her. She could hear his labored breathing getting closer to her. *Huff, huff.* She ran to the closest edge of the roof that she could reach since she knew she couldn't make it to the front of the school before he caught her. She slowed for a second when she reached the edge but she really had no time to hesitate. She closed her eyes, felt the wind and just fell right off the building into the wind just as she felt the hand of the hooded figure graze her hair and her jersey. She opened her eyes and luckily she saw the wind and glided along with it. Thankfully, this part of the school was only one story because this was pretty high for Evie to jump off of. She landed a little harder than she had when practicing this with her uncle Cy and she rolled a little bit. She didn't have time to even think about whether she was okay or not. She started running to the front of the school. She never looked back to see if the hooded guy was still following her or not. She didn't stop until she reached the almost empty front parking lot where her parents were waiting for her. They saw her and immediately started running towards her. They knew something was wrong.

"What happened? Where were you? Are you okay? Why haven't you changed?" Her parents were both frantically asking her questions.

"Mom, Dad! I can't believe it! I'm so sorry. I just talked to Logan for a few minutes and I…"

"Wait, honey, slow down," her dad said as he could tell Evie needed to catch her breath.

Evie explained everything to them and told them again she was so sorry. They were upset with her for not following their instructions but they knew it had scared her so bad that she had learned her lesson. And actually, they were more upset over the fact that this person was still after her and would go so far as to try and attack her at the school. They knew they needed to be even more careful and more vigilant. They went with Evie to the locker room to get her stuff. Noah looked all around but there was no sign of the hooded figure. They debated whether to call the police and ultimately decided to do so. By this time, they were the only people left at the school, which made Evie happy so that no one would find out about this incident. The police arrived promptly but there was nothing they could do. They questioned Evie and made a report of it but she never even saw the person's face, so there wasn't much to go on.

After that, on the ride home, there was much discussion about how to further protect Evie and how to keep someone with her at all times. Evie's first reaction was to be angry that she needed to depend on others so much. She didn't want to lose even more of her independence than she had already lost. She worried that this would keep her from doing anything outside of school and the ability to do anything with Logan or her friends. But if she was honest with herself, she wasn't that angry about it. After this scary incident, she was relieved to hear plans to keep her safe. She finally realized how serious this was and that her parents were not just being overprotective. She also finally accepted this new reality of never being alone. She knew she would have to have an adult with her at all times and she actually wanted it that way. It felt like her life would never be the same again. She swallowed hard trying not to cry. It was no good. The tears started rolling down her cheeks almost in rivers. *Why was this happening?* She felt like this was so unfair. She hadn't asked for this and it was altering her whole life. The fear she had felt when running from the hooded man also really hit her. Her parents tried to console her and talked to her the whole way home trying to make her feel better. They vowed they would protect her and told her she would still see her friends. By the time Evie got home she had stopped crying, but she was still feeling scared. Her parents stayed with her until she fell asleep. Rose and Noah then stayed up for a while discussing how scary this was and what to do next.

The next day, Evie's parents were still at a loss over how to handle things. They were sure that Evie would never be alone again and they repeatedly told her she was never to put herself in a situation like that ever again.

"You have to be more careful. Not more careful, the most careful you can possibly be. Never be alone. Never separate yourself from a group," her dad went on and on.

"I know I made a mistake," Evie said. "I won't let it happen again."

"Well, we are going to make sure it doesn't ever happen again," Rose said. "I called Cy and he is coming over to discuss how to better watch over you."

"No! We don't need a big family meeting about me! We can keep things the way they are! I just screwed up! I promise I'll be more careful," Evie said.

"I don't feel like you understand how serious this is, Evie," her mom continued. "You could have died. You could die. This person is out to kill you. They don't care about you or your family or anything. We believe this person wants to end the elf people and will do anything they can to achieve this. So, yes, we need a family meeting. This person is obviously not giving up and they are going to try again. So, Cy, your dad and I will be a part of your life even more than we already are."

Evie opened her mouth to complain, but her dad interrupted her.

"Don't try to argue, Evie," her dad said. "This is too serious. We are just trying to protect you. What happened last night was way too close. I can't believe he got that close to hurting you. We have to do a better job. I thought we were doing a pretty good job, but obviously not. Now we will do better."

Evie didn't argue. She knew that this was serious. She didn't say it, but she agreed that her parents were right. She could have been killed last night. She realized she needed the chaperones.

"Okay," Evie said to her parents. "I know this is serious. I'll go along with whatever you guys feel like we need to do. I think, probably."

Just then, Cy and Rion arrived at the door and came in. Cy immediately hugged Evie.

"I'm so glad you're okay," Cy said as he kept Evie in a hug. "Thank goodness we practiced your gliding so much."

Cy finally let Evie go and she said, "Yeah, thank goodness we did."

"I can't believe what happened, Evie," Rion said. "It's beyond scary. This seems so real now. Are you okay?"

"I'm fine, I guess. Actually, it was really scary. I guess I'm still a little scared," Evie answered honestly.

"Well, I imagine," Cy added. "I can't believe this guy tried to hurt you again. And right at the school. He is getting more determined; more desperate. Something has to change. We need to find this guy. We need to get this guy."

"Yes, we do," Noah added. "The sooner, the better."

"We need to figure out who this guy is," Cy said. "It may be someone we already know. Do you remember anything about him, Evie? Is there anything you can tell us about him?"

"I couldn't see his face," Evie answered. "He had a hoodie on and he had the hood pulled down low, like over half his face. I could sorta see his mouth and chin but there wasn't anything special about it or anything that would set him apart from anyone else."

"Did he have any facial hair," Cy asked.

"No, I don't think so. But I barely saw him because I was mostly just running from him. I doubt I would even recognize him if I saw him without the hood…" she kind of trailed off a little as a feeling came over her. "But for some reason," she continued, "I feel like there was something familiar about him. I don't know what though. I can't pinpoint what exactly was familiar about him. But I feel like I've seen him before."

"See, just as I said. I think it's someone we know, or at least some kind of acquaintance. What was his body type like?" Cy asked.

"He was tall. He was probably just over six feet. But other than that, he was normal looking," Evie told them.

"We've asked her this over and over," Rose said. "We wish we could figure out who this guy is too. We also keep wondering if it is someone we know. Or someone Evie knows. We have to be suspicious of everyone."

"And like we were saying, Evie, things will change some more. I'm sorry about this but it's necessary. Never be alone again. And you won't be going out too much or to anyone else's house," Noah added.

"Wait, what?" Evie asked, suddenly confused. "I have to go over to Logan's to finish our project. It's due soon."

"Then Logan can come over here," her dad continued. "This is not up for discussion. Logan will have to come here and that is that."

"But we've already planned for me to go over there. It'll seem weird if I suddenly ask him to come over here."

"No, it won't. Just tell him that your parents want to see your project and blame it on us, okay?" Rose said. "It has to be this way, Evie. I'm sorry but it has to be." Rose felt bad as Evie looked miserable. "Don't worry," she added, "we promise to do our very best to let you see your friends and still have some fun. This has always been our goal. Your friends can just come over here more now, including Logan."

Evie knew there was no point in arguing. She hated that this was happening but she believed them that they would do their best to keep her life as normal as possible. "So, what's next then?" she asked.

"I think two of us should be at all of Evie's games and practices," Cy said. "One or hopefully, two of us will be taking you to school every day, Evie and picking you up. You will mostly have to hang out here when you want to see your friends. I'm sorry but the biggest change is that going out will be limited. And if you do go out, you will have at least two of us there as chaperones. That way there can be two sets of eyes looking around for this person. I know it's a lot, but it is necessary."

"Sounds terrible, but okay, I guess," Evie said reluctantly. "I understand."

"I'm so sorry, sweetie," Rose said as her dad also came over to comfort her. "I know this is not what you wanted, this is not what anyone wants, but we have to do what we have to do."

Cy and Rion had to go and Evie just wanted to be alone for a while, so she went to her room. She felt sorry for herself for a little while but decided that was a waste of time and so she decided to just move on and pretend life was normal. She really wanted to see Kat so she texted her to see if she could come over and hang out sometime over the weekend. Evie wanted to tell Kat about everything that had happened because Kat still didn't know about the guy who chased her after the game. Evie hadn't talked to Kat since she stayed with Logan while Kat went to change with the rest of the team. But Kat never texted back all weekend, which was strange because Kat always texted Evie back. Evie wondered why she didn't respond. This made Evie anxious to see Kat at school on Monday.

CHAPTER 6

THE QUARREL & THE TALK

Evie had her parents bring her to school a little early on Monday morning. She sat in the classroom of first period, History, waiting for Kat to come in. She sat and waited the entire extra time there was as Kat was usually early but Kat didn't walk in until right as the bell was ringing. She walked straight to her desk and didn't even look at Evie. Evie knew something was wrong and History seemed to take forever that morning as Evie waited to find out what her friend was upset about. When the class was finally over, Evie got up to stand in front of Kat to confront her but suddenly Logan appeared in front of Evie to talk to her. Kat walked past them both and Evie heard her say, "Typical." Rion knew that Kat hadn't replied to Evie's texts all weekend as Evie had told him and she hadn't replied to his texts either, so he went after Kat to find out what was wrong as Evie stayed with Logan.

"Hey," Logan said. "How was your weekend?"

"Oh, fine," Evie replied, not really focused on what Logan had said, since she was paying attention to Kat right now and completely forgetting that she had had the encounter with the guy who chased her Friday night. She realized she was distracted when Kat was out of sight and looked back at Logan. "How was your weekend?"

"Kinda boring," Logan replied. "So, I know we're almost done with our president presentation but I thought we should get together one more time to finalize everything before it's due next week. Can you come over sometime this week or this weekend?"

"Oh yeah," Evie just remembered her weekend and everything that had happened. "I was wondering if you could come over to my house. My parents wanted to see our project. I know it's kind of lame, but…"

"Oh no, that would be fine," Logan interjected as he was glad to be invited over to Evie's house. "How about on Saturday? I can ask my parents tonight."

"Yeah, I will talk to my parents too," Evie said. "It's nice that we're so close to done with this project."

"Yeah, it is," Logan replied even though he liked working on the project with Evie and he wished it wasn't ending. They both stood there for a second and no one said anything. Evie was still thinking about Kat. "So, I'll talk to you later, I guess," Logan said. He could tell that Evie seemed distracted.

"Okay, cool," Evie said. "Talk to you later."

Evie and Logan left the classroom and went separate ways for their next class. Evie wished she could run and find Kat but she knew that she didn't have time to find her and talk to her. It wasn't until lunch that Evie would see Kat again and by that time, she had a good guess as to why Kat was mad. She didn't blame her for being mad either. She figured Kat was upset that Evie was spending so much time with Logan and especially that Evie had left Kat's company to talk to Logan after their last game. Evie felt terrible. She knew that Kat was particularly upset that evening about missing the goal that lost them the game and she realized that she should have stayed with her friend to console her. Evie felt like she was a bad friend and Kat had always been such a good friend. Kat deserved better and Evie was ready to tell her so when she saw her next.

It felt like it took forever to get to lunch, but when the time finally came, Evie headed straight towards Kat hoping Kat would not walk away from her or not listen to her. As Evie approached Kat, she was ready to insist on being heard, when Kat suddenly threw her arms around Evie and hugged her.

"I can't believe what happened to you. Oh my gosh, that is so scary. I'm so glad you're okay," Kat said as she slowly let go of Evie. "Rion told me what happened after the game with the scary, mystery guy chasing you," Kat explained as Evie looked a little confused.

"Oh yeah, that."

"What do you mean, 'Oh yeah, that,'?" Kat exclaimed. "Just a little thing, of someone trying to kill you!"

"No, I know, it's completely serious," Evie said. "I was just confused because I thought you were mad at me and I totally understand why and I was about to apologize and…"

"Evie, take a breath, girl. I was mad, but now I'm just glad you're okay. It was just a small thing and I wasn't super mad, just a little mad. Mostly I think I was upset about losing the game and then it was convenient to focus that on you. Well, I was mad at you too though for…"

"For leaving you when you were upset and for not being a good friend," Evie added. "I am so sorry. I'm going to do better and not leave you when you need me. I should've stayed with you."

"Thanks, Evie," Kat said. "That means a lot to me. Thanks for seeing that you should've stayed with me. I know it's hard when your crush is standing there waiting for you and wants to talk to you," Kat said with a smile.

"Whatever!" Evie replied. "He's not my crush! I mean, I like him and he's a good friend. I mean, we've been hanging out more," Evie was starting to trail off as her next thought hit her but then she just blurted it out. "But I don't even know how he feels. I guess his brother did say that he likes me, but he could've meant just as a friend."

Kat was just smiling and giving Evie a look like she knows she likes Logan, so she might as well admit it.

"Okay," Evie owned up. "I like him more than a friend. Stop looking at me!"

Evie and Kat both started laughing just as Rion walked up and joined them.

"Oh good, you guys are back to normal. You are, right?" Rion asked them and they both nodded yes. "I told Kat everything that happened, Evie. I hope that was okay," Rion said looking to Evie.

"Yes, definitely," Evie replied. "I'm glad you did. I was going to tell her anyway. And I'm just happy that things are good with us again."

"Me too," Kat replied. "And all it took was someone trying to attack you," Kat said as a joke. "But seriously, that is so crazy! I can't believe this guy tried to attack you right here at the school. I can't believe this is all real. You must be terrified. How are you? Are you okay?"

"I'm fine. I mean, I guess I'm fine. I really don't know what to think about it. It doesn't seem real. I'm just thankful that Uncle Cy had taught me how to jump off the roof or else I wouldn't have gotten away. It's really scary to think of that. I'm still a little scared. Mom and Dad won't let me be alone and I'm kinda glad about it. It's sort of annoying but if I'm honest, I don't want to be alone."

"I wouldn't either," Kat said. "That is so scary to think of what could've happened."

"Yeah, I'm so glad dad taught you how to fly or whatever you call it," Rion said. "He was too, but seriously, stay with your team after practice and after your next game. Don't give this guy the opportunity."

"I know, I know. It was really dumb of me to separate from the group," Evie admitted.

"But Logan was waiting," Kat said with a funny tone. "And Evie loves Logan."

"Oh, stop it, I don't love him."

"Well, we know you like him," Rion said.

"Oh, yes, she finally admitted it. She likes him," Kat said as she continued to give Evie funny looks while Evie looked a little shy and unsure of herself. Seeing this, Kat added, "and everyone knows he likes her too."

"Everyone does not know that," Evie quipped back. "I don't know that. I wish I did," Evie said as she stared at the floor.

"Oh come on, Evie. He definitely likes you," Kat said as Rion nodded in agreement. "I know he does, there is no doubt. And from what you told me, I think his brother already told you that he likes you; more than a friend."

"Well, I guess I hope he does," Evie admitted. "But how will I ever know? It's not like I'm gonna ask him or anything."

"I think something will happen soon that will tell you or show you that he likes you," Kat said.

"I think he already shows that he likes you," Rion added as he gave a look to Kat. "He asked you to be his partner, he has asked you to his house and to movies and stuff, he comes to all of your games. You just want more to show you. But it's harder than you think for a guy to show a girl that he likes her," Rion said as he looked at Kat again.

"I just want to know for sure," Evie said.

"Just give it time, Evie," Kat said.

"Yeah, okay. I guess I have to. Hopefully, something will happen soon."

"It will," Kat said.

Evie, Kat and Rion spent the rest of lunch talking and laughing and Evie managed to not think much about the hooded guy for the rest of the day thanks to her best friends.

When Evie first woke up the next morning, she was in a great mood. Not only were things all better with Kat, Logan was coming over that weekend to finish up their project. She was feeling great until all of a sudden when thoughts of the hooded guy came flooding back. She remembered his tall, menacing stance and the thought of him running after her and gaining on her. Suddenly, fear and a huge amount of anxiety surged through her like an electric shock. She could barely breathe and her heart was racing. The anxiety was in her chest and it felt like she would never feel normal again. The thoughts of that night had been hitting her many times since it happened but until now those thoughts had only given her brief anxiety. Knowing that her family members were all there to protect her and were not going to leave her alone had helped relieve the anxiety and fear. This time was different though. She couldn't make it stop. She kept telling herself that she was okay and that everyone was going to keep her safe, but the overwhelming feeling of fear and anxiety would not let up. She didn't know what to do. This feeling was scaring her and she did not like feeling this way. She sat there for a while hoping it would go away but after it wouldn't, she decided to go tell her parents about it.

"Mom! Dad!" she yelled.

"What's wrong?" her mom yelled back as she could tell something was bothering her daughter and it was odd for Evie to yell for them in the morning.

"Do you guys have a minute?" Evie replied. "I know the morning is crazy and we usually don't have much time, but could we talk?"

"Of course," said her father. Noah looked at Rose with a worried look. Evie saw this and felt bad to make them worry.

"I don't want y'all to worry. I guess I'm just feeling a little off," Evie continued.

"What do you mean, 'off'?" Noah asked.

"Well, it's like I have this feeling in my chest or something," Evie replied. "I woke up feeling fine and then things changed when I remembered the other night with the hooded guy. And I don't know, I could barely breathe all of a sudden and I felt scared and some other feeling that does not feel good. I don't know what to call it or how to describe it."

"It sounds like anxiety," Rose said with a concerned look. Evie noticed this look and got even more scared. Rose realized she was making things worse for Evie so she shifted her tone. "Don't worry, sweetie, lots of people suffer with anxiety. Not to say it's a little thing, because it's not, I know. It is very uncomfortable and can be very difficult to deal with. But there are different treatments. What I'm trying to say is that there is help for it." Rose was struggling and felt like she was not helping. Noah stepped in to help her.

"Well, it's not a surprise that you would feel scared or anxious, Evie," Noah said. "You went through a huge thing, something that most people never go through and something that would scare anyone. I'm sorry that you're feeling anxious, I have felt that before and it's not a good feeling. It's miserable. Has it been happening very often?"

"I dunno," Evie replied. "It happens sometimes. But not like this, like not this bad. I feel like I am too scared to even leave the house. And yeah, I guess it's been happening kinda often. It's like the memories of that night just hit me all of a sudden and it puts this feeling in my chest and stomach. It's like I'm reliving it all over again."

"Like your dad said, it's not a surprise for you to feel this way," her mom added. "What you went through was terrible and honestly I would be surprised if you didn't feel something like this. We need to do something about it. I don't want to just ignore this. We can't ignore this, especially if you feel scared to leave the house."

"What can we do?" Evie asked.

"I think you should go and see a therapist," Rose said as she saw Evie make a face, like there was no way she was doing that. "Now, hold on," Rose continued, "don't jump to conclusions or make a decision without knowing any information."

"A therapist?" Evie interjected. "That sounds like an overreaction. I don't need a therapist. I'm not crazy."

"Whoa," Noah said. "Going to a therapist is a completely normal thing. It definitely does not mean you are crazy. Plenty of people go to therapists for a variety of different reasons and it by no means, should make you think that a person is crazy or think any different of a person for going to therapy."

"I would just feel like a weirdo or something," Evie said. "I would be embarrassed."

"You shouldn't feel like a weirdo or feel embarrassed," Noah said. "Therapy can be really helpful and should be seen as a positive thing."

"We wouldn't have to tell anyone," Rose said. "We know a therapist who is a good friend. We would trust him to keep our secret, so you could actually tell him the whole story. I think it would be really healthy for you to talk to someone. Just think about it."

"Okay," said Evie.

"Can you push yourself to go to school today?" Rose asked.

"I think so," Evie answered.

Evie thought about the therapist idea all day and still felt weird about it. She wanted so bad to talk to someone else about seeing a therapist but she didn't want to tell anyone. She had never kept a secret from Rion or Kat before, but she decided to not tell them about this. She would have to figure this one out on her own. As she kept feeling afraid throughout the day and having bouts of anxiety swelling in her chest, she decided on her own that it might be a good idea to talk to someone. She just wanted to do something about the way she was feeling and this was the only answer she had right now. She wanted to feel better.

That evening she told her mom and dad that she was okay with going to see this therapist that they knew. Her mom called the next morning and made an appointment for that Friday morning. The appointment was super early in the morning so that it would be before school. Evie just decided that she would keep an open mind about this but she also decided she would not tell anyone about it. She told her mom and dad not to tell anyone and especially for her mom not to tell Cy as he might tell Rion.

On Friday morning, the alarm went off so early that it was really hard to get up. Her windows were covered in dew and she thought to herself that even the windows looked sleepy. By the time she got to her appointment she was more awake but she was nervous and apprehensive about the whole thing. Her mom and dad took her to it and her mom walked in with her to introduce her.

"Hi, Evan," Rose said as she greeted the therapist. "Thanks

for seeing Evie so soon and so early."

"Oh, it's my pleasure," he responded. "I just hope that I can help."

"Evie, this is Mr. Dancy," Rose said as Mr. Dancy stuck out his hand to shake Evie's hand.

"It's nice to meet you," Evie said.

"You too," Mr. Dancy replied. "Well, should we get started?"

"Already?" Evie asked feeling a little nervous.

"We can take a little time if that makes you more comfortable. Your mom can stay if you want," Mr. Dancy said.

"Everything will be fine, Evie," Rose said. "You just have to talk. But if you want me to stay, I will."

Evie thought about it and realized she wanted to do this on her own. "No, that's okay," she said. "I can do this."

"Okay, good. Let me get out of the way then. I will just be out in the car with your dad, if you need me," Rose said to Evie and then turned to Mr. Dancy. "Thanks again, Evan."

"It was nice to see you, Rose," Mr. Dancy said.

"Have a seat," Mr. Dancy said as he and Evie both sat down. "I want you to feel as comfortable and relaxed as you can. Why don't you start with telling me about how you feel when these unwanted feelings come in."

Evie did her best to describe what she had been feeling. It wasn't easy to describe these feelings and she felt a little awkward telling them to a stranger.

"Well, when it starts, I just suddenly remember the night and the guy who was chasing me and it's like there's this bubble of fear that goes off," Evie started. "I feel so scared sometimes, I feel like I can't move. It usually starts to ease up as I think about things and sort of, you know, talk myself down. But then I'm left with this anxiety, or whatever, I guess that's what you call it. I don't like the way it feels. It's hard to describe. It's like there's this tightness around my heart and lungs."

"Okay," the therapist said when she stopped. "You're doing well. We will talk more later about your anxiety and some things you can do when that happens to try and make yourself feel better. Now, do you feel up to telling me about the night that this incident happened? Can you tell me the whole story? I know it may be hard to talk about, but if you can, I would really like for you to."

"Okay," said Evie. She tried hard to tell the whole story and not leave out any details. It definitely wasn't easy to do so. Just saying it all out loud made her feel a ton of anxiety and fear. She kept having to take deep breaths and pausing here and there. The therapist would take these moments to encourage her and tell her she was doing a good job. It took longer than she thought it would to tell everything.

"Now, how did telling that story make you feel?" the therapist asked.

"It made me feel scared. And I guess the anxiety again; like a lot," Evie answered as another thought hit her. "But it made me feel angry too though. I mean I don't understand how this guy, who doesn't even know me, can want to kill me. How can he feel that way about me when I haven't done anything to him? It just doesn't make any sense to me. How could you want to hurt someone you don't even know? I just want to know who he is. I mean maybe I do know him. Maybe he does have a reason to not like me or something. But even so, I know I haven't done anything to deserve what he is doing. I haven't done anything to deserve to be killed."

"Yes, you are correct about that," Mr. Dancy said. "Is that what makes you feel angry?"

"Yes," said Evie.

"Tell me more about that," Mr. Dancy said.

"It makes me feel angry and confused and..." She paused for a minute. "And helpless. I feel like there is nothing I can do. Like, if I could just talk to the guy maybe I could make him feel differently. I could tell him that just because I'm an elf doesn't mean I deserve to be killed. I just found out I'm an elf and I'm still the same person that I was before. So, just being an elf isn't a good reason to want to kill me. I just wish there was something I could do to change how he feels."

"Well, that would probably be hard since we don't know who he is," the therapist added. "But over time, it may be discovered who he is. Once he is discovered, maybe with some time, he can be convinced to feel differently."

"I hope so," Evie said. "I mean, it's like part of me feels bad for this guy because he's obviously hurting about something. I wish I could make him feel better so that would lead to him not wanting to hurt me."

"That shows much compassion, Evie," Mr. Dancy said, "to actually feel bad for this man and want to help him. Try to focus on that compassion when you're feeling anxious. This may help alleviate the unwanted feelings."

"I also feel mad at him, though," Evie said.

"That is completely fine and expected," Mr. Dancy said. "You should feel mad. You don't have to try and push away that feeling. Let it happen. But as best as you can, focus on the compassion for your own wellbeing. My suggestion to focus on the compassion is only to benefit you and to take away your discomfort."

Evie and Mr. Dancy talked for the entire hour and it flew by. Before she left, Mr. Dancy gave her some activities to do to help alleviate her anxiety. She thanked him for seeing her and said yes, she would like to come back when he asked her. Evie's mom came back in to get her and they made an appointment to come back the next week at the same time. Evie was surprised how much better she felt when she left his office and it even continued in the car with her parents as they drove her to school.

CHAPTER 7

THE QUESTION & THE DRESS

Evie felt strange not telling Kat and Rion about her morning. It felt weird having a secret from them but it wasn't something she felt comfortable sharing yet. Though her attitude regarding therapy was already completely different, she still wanted to keep it to herself. She didn't quite understand why though since it really wasn't as embarrassing to her as it initially was. Therapy definitely wasn't as odd as she thought it was going to be. It was pretty normal actually and it felt like the right thing to do. It was just talking but somehow it made her feel better. Therapy turned out to be a great tool in helping with her anxiety. When Kat and Rion walked into class together, Evie felt like she was wearing her secret on her sleeve. She couldn't think of how to act normal towards them and she thought they would know something was up for sure. She started smiling at them as they walked up and suddenly realized she didn't have a clue what to say, when Rion took the pressure off of her.

"Hey, Superman, jumped off any tall buildings lately?" Rion said to Evie.

"Rion! That's not funny," Kat scolded him.

"No, that's hilarious," Evie said as she started laughing and feeling the worry melt away from her. *In fact, it's perfect*, she thought. This was exactly what Evie needed to help forget about her secret and just be normal towards her friends. It also helped her act normal when Logan walked into the classroom. They exchanged long smiles at each other before both realizing they were staring at one another and quickly looking away.

The day went by slow for Evie since she was excited about the weekend and hanging out with Logan. She confirmed with Logan that he was coming over to her house on Saturday and he said he was looking forward to it. That made her feel very happy to know she wasn't the only one looking forward to it. Getting together outside of school was how they had mostly gotten to know each other since they didn't have much time to talk in their classes and they didn't have lunch together and she wanted to continue to get to know Logan.

It was finally Saturday afternoon and Logan arrived at Evie's house right on time. Evie's parents were very happy to see him again and to get to know him better. They had met him before and they had seen him at Evie's games but they didn't really know him. Being around him this time, they got a better sense of what kind of a person he was. Rose and Noah thought he was very nice and polite and they approved of their friendship. Rose and Noah were also glad to see the project they had been working on. Logan had brought all the materials for their project. They were making a tri fold poster board to be the main part of their presentation. They really were almost done, so they didn't have much work to take up their time. For most of the two hours, they just talked and hung out.

"So, how's soccer practices been going?" Logan asked.

"It's been good," Evie said as she remembered the last time Logan saw her play which was the awful night with the incident. She took a deep breath and Logan noticed.

"What? Is something wrong? Something about soccer?" Logan asked.

"Oh, no," Evie replied. She realized what she had done and

wasn't sure how to answer him. She couldn't tell him about what really happened, though she wanted to, so she searched her brain for something else to say. The first thing she thought of was her fight with Kat. "I just had a fight with Kat after that last game we lost. It's over now and we're fine, but I hated it while it was going on. But like I said, we're all good now, so it's cool." She wasn't sure Kat would like her telling Logan about this, so she tried to just gloss over it. It didn't work.

"What? That surprises me. I didn't think you and Kat ever had a fight. What was it about?" Logan asked the very question Evie hoped he wouldn't.

"Uh, er, it was about," Evie was trying to think of something to say but being that she wasn't a very good liar, she couldn't think of anything. "It was about you, actually." *Oh no*, Evie thought. She couldn't believe she just told him that.

"Oh," said Logan, who was very surprised. "Well, that's not good. I don't want to cause any fights between you guys."

"Well, it's nothing you did on purpose," Evie tried to explain. "I can't even believe I just told you this. Please don't give it much thought or anything. It's really not a big deal. It was just that I stayed with you instead of her when we had just lost and everything. I should've stayed with her when she was upset. But it didn't last long. She wasn't even that mad. She was just upset about the loss and that just made things worse. But seriously, we are totally good now."

"Okay, good. I'm sorry I took you away from her after the game," Logan said.

"No, really, you don't need to be sorry," Evie said. "You didn't do anything wrong."

"I just wanted to see you and try to cheer you up after the loss," Logan replied.

"I wanted to see you too. You did cheer me up." Evie thought her cheeks may be turning red after saying this so she tried to keep talking. "Kat understood, she was just bummed about the loss. I told her that I should've stayed with her and I told her I was sorry. That made her feel better and she completely forgave me. I think the main problem was that she really blamed herself for the loss."

"Yeah, I feel for her," Logan said, who was also an athlete. "I hate to lose too, especially when you feel like it was your fault. But I can't wait to be playing baseball again."

"I can't wait to see some of your games," Evie said, trying to change the subject. "It'll be my turn to watch you play instead of you watching me play." Evie became aware that this sounded like something a girlfriend would say or do and she quickly added, "I mean, if you want me to watch and come see your games."

"Of course I do," Logan said and Evie's face broke into a huge smile.

"Good," Evie added. "It'll be nice to return the favor of watching your games since you've seen so many of my games. It's fun to hang out and it's kind of like hanging out together. I mean, we're kind of together. But I guess it's more fun when we're actually together." Evie was starting to ramble.

"Yeah, well," Logan said and Evie could tell he suddenly seemed nervous. This made her nervous too as she thought maybe she said too much and that she enjoyed their time together more than he did. Logan continued, "Speaking of being together… I was wondering, I mean, I have wanted to ask you…" Logan paused and Evie was curious as to what he was going to ask her. He was noticeably uncomfortable. "Well, you might know, or you might not know, I'm not sure… uh, that there's…

uh, a dance at the school in a couple of weeks." Evie got even more nervous but happy too, seeing where this was heading. "There's like a dance or whatever," Logan continued, "and I was wondering if…you would like to go with me?" Logan suddenly started speaking very fast and Evie could barely make out this last sentence. She wanted to make sure that he really did ask her so she didn't assume it.

"What was that last part?" Evie asked and Logan realized he had rushed through it.

"Uh, would you like to go to the dance with me?" Logan said very clearly.

Evie felt relieved that this was what he was saying. She also couldn't believe he was asking her this. It was just as Kat had said that something would happen soon to show her that Logan liked her and now it was happening. Evie was so happy, but she tried to keep her cool and not geek out over this moment. "Um, yes, I would like to go to the dance with you," she casually replied. "That sounds like a lot of fun."

"Oh good," Logan said as he seemed relieved. "I didn't know what you would say. Especially after…" Logan suddenly trailed off.

"Especially after what?" Evie asked.

"Never mind, I shouldn't have even said anything," Logan replied.

"No, come on, tell me what you were going to say," Evie said.

"It's just that my brother said that he ran into you at the park and he got the impression that you didn't really like me. Or that you only thought I was nice or something," Logan said.

"Oh," Evie said. "Yeah, I did see him at the park but I didn't mean that I didn't like you by what I said." Evie couldn't think of what to say next. She wanted to say that she did like Logan but she thought that was a little too much and anyway, she was too shy to say that. She tried to reassure Logan by saying, "Your brother just… got it wrong."

"Oh, okay. Good. Carter was probably just trying to cause trouble." Logan realized he wanted to change the subject. "So, I'm sure my parents will be cool with it. I guess I will have to wear a tie or something."

"Oh yeah," Evie said as she thought about her parents and wondered if they would even let her go. "I think my parents will let me go too. I will have to ask them. I guess this means I will have to get a dress?" This was the only bad thing about this new development as Evie wasn't that big on wearing dresses.

"Yeah, you might," Logan answered. "I've never seen you in a dress before."

"I don't wear them very often," Evie replied. "But I will for the dance."

"Well, that makes me feel special," Logan said and they both laughed.

"I wonder if Kat and Rion are going to go," Evie thought aloud. "We could go as a group," Evie said, but as she said it she could tell Logan wasn't thrilled about this idea. "Or not," she quickly said. "We should go, just the two of us."

"That sounds good to me," Logan confirmed her suspicion.

"We will just have to figure out whose parents will drive us and all that," Logan added. "I know my parents are going to want pictures, so we may have to go to my house or let them come over here or something. I hope it's not too complicated."

"My parents will probably want pictures too. So, it will probably be complicated," Evie said and they both laughed again. "Maybe we can just all meet here and take pictures before we go.

My parents will probably want to drive us," Evie said as she remembered her parents' rules about being with her everywhere she goes.

"Sounds good," Logan said. "I'm already looking forward to it."

"Me, too," Evie said with a small smile and look at Logan and he returned it.

Evie was preparing to ask her parents about going to the dance and noticed she was biting her finger nails a little too much. Under normal conditions, she would be a little nervous to ask being that it was her first date or sort-of-date with a boy but she was especially nervous to ask because she was worried that they would say no because of the situation and the danger surrounding her. She timidly approached them to first scope out their mood and likelihood of being agreeable.

"Hey, guys," Evie said to her parents as she walked into the kitchen.

"Hey there, sweetie," her dad replied. "How did things go with you and Logan? Did you finish your project?"

"Yeah, we finished," Evie responded. "We're all set for next week to present it. We feel good about it."

"Well, that's good. I'm glad you two finished it," her mom replied. "Logan is a really sweet kid. Your dad and I were happy to see him again today. He is so nice and polite. I'm glad you were assigned to be partners with him."

"Actually, we weren't assigned as partners," Evie said. "He asked me to be his partner. I don't think he really knew anyone in the class since he was new and me, Kat and Rion were having trouble figuring out who would be partners with who and he just walked up and asked. It was kind of surprising." Evie couldn't help but smile a little saying this and both of her parents noticed this and smiled at each other.

"Well, it all worked out then, didn't it?" Rose said. "Logan saved you, Kat and Rion from some awkwardness it sounds like."

"Yeah, I guess," Evie said and her parents noticed she now seemed distracted.

"What's going on in that head of yours?" Noah asked.

"What?" Evie said, suddenly looking up. "Oh. Well, speaking of Logan asking me things… um… today he asked me something else… something I need to talk to you guys about."

"Okay," Rose said. Evie wasn't responding right away so Rose continued, "Well, what is it? Just spit it out, don't be nervous."

"Uh, Logan, today, asked me… if I would want to go to the dance with him. See, there's this dance coming up at school in two weeks and Logan asked if I wanted to go with him." Evie felt good to finally get it all out.

"Oh, okay," Noah said. "I'm not sure how I feel about that. I feel like you are a little young to have a date."

"It's not a date," Evie said. "Everyone from school will be there. I'm sure Kat and Rion will be going too. I haven't asked them yet, but I'm sure they will be. There will be teachers and stuff there too."

"I remember going to a dance with a boy when I was Evie's age," Rose said. "So, it's not really that young." Rose looked at Noah to see what he was thinking. "You always say that you want Evie to have a normal childhood and this is part of having a normal childhood. I think it would be okay for her to go. What I am more worried about is," Rose said looking back at Evie, "that you are not alone at all during the dance. You must be very careful and stay with the group at all times. Don't even go to the bathroom alone. And your dad and I will be driving you to the dance and picking you up, no debate about that."

"So, I can go?" Evie asked.

Rose looked at Noah and he nodded his head.

"Yes, you can go," Rose said.

Evie's face broke out in a huge smile. "Thank you, thank you, thank you! I figured you guys would want to drive and Logan was saying that his parents would want pictures so I was thinking maybe we could all meet here and do pictures and then you guys could drive us to the dance. Would that work?"

"Sounds good to us," Noah said. "I can't believe my little girl is going to a school dance. You are growing up so fast."

"Oh, Dad, don't get all cheesy," Evie said. "It's just a dance."

"Okay, okay," Noah said.

"So, Mom," Evie said, "I guess I will need a dress. I don't really want to wear a dress, but I guess I should."

"Ohhh," her mom replied. "Yay! I get to help you pick out a dress! I didn't think about that. This is going to be so much fun!"

"Now it's your turn to stop being all cheesy," Evie said to her mom. "It's just a dress. Let's not make a big deal of it."

"Okay," Rose replied. "But yes, I will take you shopping for a dress." Rose couldn't help but let a huge smile spread across her face. She rarely got to do anything girly with Evie.

Rose thought they should go shopping the next day, Sunday, but Evie was convinced it would only take one day, so she wanted to wait until the next Saturday. Rose convinced her it may take more time and they should play it safe, so they ventured out the next day to go to a few stores that Rose had in mind.

"I won't need to go to a few stores," Evie said. "I will find something at the first store, I know it."

"Sure you will," Rose said. "You don't realize how hard it is going to be to find just the right dress."

"I just don't think it'll be that hard," Evie said.

"Well, we'll see," Rose said.

At the first store, things did not go as well as Evie thought they would. It was fine at first as Evie liked so many of them on the rack. She and her mom picked out a few dresses to try on and Evie went to the changing room. Her mom stood outside and waited until her daughter was ready with the first dress.

After waiting for longer than she thought it would take, Rose asked, "Are you okay in there, sweetie? Did you try on the first dress?"

"Yes," said Evie with a huge sigh, "and it's awful. I look terrible."

"Well, let me see," said Rose.

"No!" Evie said. "I'm not showing anyone this dress. I look so weird."

"I'm sure you don't look weird," Rose said. "I really think you should let me see. We are all our own worst critic."

"What does that even mean?" Evie asked.

"It means that we are most critical of ourselves and that we are way more critical of ourselves than other people are critical of us. Especially of how we look," Rose answered. "I want you to be less critical of yourself and learn to love how you look."

"Love how I look?" Evie replied. "There is no way I can love how I look in this dress."

"What is so wrong with it?" Rose asked. "Please, can I just see it?"

"Okay," said Evie. "I will let you see. Is there anyone else out there?"

"No," said Rose.

So, Evie stepped out of the dressing room and her mother honestly thought that she looked adorable.

"You look so cute," Rose said. "I promise that I am not just saying that. I really mean it."

"Well, I think I look terrible," Evie said. "I don't like this dress. I just hope that it's the dress making me look so weird. I mean, what is up with my collar bone? Has it always stuck out like this?"

"You don't look weird. But I'm sure it is just the dress, so try on the next one," Rose said. "Don't waste time on one that you don't love."

Evie tried on two more dresses and did not like either of them. She continued to say that she looked weird, or that her shoulders looked weird in one or that her knees looked weird in another. She even thought one made her neck look too long. Every dress made her focus on one of her body parts and she noticed things about herself that she had never noticed before. Had she always been so gangly?

"I am so awkward," Evie said. "I mean, really, this is ridiculous."

They decided to go a different store. Things did not go better at the next store though. Evie was overly critical of herself and thought that she looked terrible in all of the dresses. Her mother thought differently and truly believed that she looked wonderful in all of them. Rose just hoped that she would be able to convince Evie that she looked good in at least one of them. They moved on but unfortunately, Evie was not convinced about any of the dresses at the next store either. With three stores down, they decided to call it a day and go again the next weekend.

Evie was discouraged and thought that she might not find a dress at all. Her mom and dad encouraged her and told her she would find something.

"Just don't be too picky," her dad told her. "There's no such thing as a perfect anything. So, there won't be a perfect dress. You just have to pick out what you like the best. Not what you think is perfect."

"Okay," said Evie and she did keep this in mind.

So, the next weekend came and at the first store, they picked out four dresses for Evie to try on. She hated the first two again. But for the third one, she kind of liked it. She didn't think she looked so weird. She thought she looked a little weird but not as weird as the others and she really liked the dress. It was blue, which was her favorite color, with short sleeves that had a little ruffle to them that she liked. It covered her shoulders and collar bone and it was just a little longer than her knees and that made her feel better too.

"I actually like this one," Evie said from the dressing room.

Rose was so relieved. "Well, let's see it then," her mom said and Evie walked out for Rose to see.

"Oh, it's adorable," Rose said. "I think this is the one. It's as close to perfect as we are going to find. You look beautiful, sweetie. I love the color."

"Thanks, Mom," Evie said. "I think this is the one too. I will try on the last one just in case, but I'm pretty sure it will be a waste. I love the color too."

It was a waste of time to try on the fourth dress but at the same time it made Evie even more certain that the last one was the right dress. They even found shoes to go with it too. They finally made a purchase and Evie took home her dress for the dance. Now she was ready and she couldn't wait.

CHAPTER 8

THE DANCE & THE ACCIDENT

Normally the two weeks since Logan had asked Evie to the dance would have went by slowly because she was very much looking forward to the dance, but she had been so busy that the time went by pretty fast. Other than her dress shopping, she and Logan had given their presentation in History class. All the time they had spent together paid off because the presentation went very well and they got an A on it.

She had also had two more appointments with Mr. Dancy and those were going very well too. The therapy sessions with him had helped with her anxiety and at the end of the two weeks, she was feeling better. During the two weeks, there were still times when the memories of that night would come back to her and she would feel the anxiety again but it was getting better. The thoughts would hit her hardest first thing in the morning and at night when she was trying to fall asleep. Mr. Dancy had given her some techniques to help her when she was inundated with those memories.

One morning it was particularly bad. Evie woke up and the thoughts and images of that night just came flooding in. *Remember what Mr. Dancy said. Do your techniques*, she thought to herself. She stopped doing anything else and took deep breaths. Evie inhaled slowly and counted to five, filling her belly and then her chest with air and then she held the breath to a count of five. Lastly, she exhaled slowly to a count of five. She did this several times and it helped. Not only had the therapy sessions themselves helped her feel better but this technique Mr. Dancy had taught her had helped her several times.

Do your other techniques too, she thought. So, as Mr. Dancy had told her to do, she didn't dwell on the thoughts of that night. She tried to think of other things. She reminded herself that she was safe and protected and not in that danger anymore. She gave attention to her surroundings and made herself aware that she was in a safe place. Mr. Dancy had also told her to focus on an activity that was coming up that made her feel happy. That was an easy one for Evie and she thought about and focused on the dance that she was very excited about.

Evie was not the only one looking forward to the dance. Logan was also very excited about it. Rion and Kat were too. When Rion found out that Evie and Logan were going together, he asked Kat if she would like to go with him. She briefly paused before answering him and that was enough to make Rion nervous and question if he was doing the right thing, so he quickly added, "Oh, just as friends." So, Rion and Kat were going "just as friends." Evie told Kat about her dress that she had finally found and Kat, being more of a dress wearer, already had a dress that she was wearing. The two couples were going to meet up at the dance.

The night finally came and Logan and his parents arrived at Evie's house. Evie's parents and Logan's parents were both very happy to see each other again. Both sets of parents took pictures and equally embarrassed their child.

"You both look so cute," Logan's mom said.

"Mom!" Logan said as he rolled his eyes and whispered, "Sorry," to Evie. Evie didn't mind as she was glad it wasn't her mom saying it. She thought that too soon though.

"They do look so cute," Rose said. "Stand a little closer together."

"No, that's close enough," Noah said and now it was Evie who was rolling her eyes. She whispered, "Sorry," back to Logan.

"Thanks for calling to tell me the color of Evie's dress," Logan's mom said. "So Logan could coordinate his tie."

"Oh, you're welcome," Rose responded. "He looks very handsome with his shirt and tie."

"And Evie looks so pretty in that dress," Claire said. "Did she have trouble finding it?"

"Oh, it was a little bit of an ordeal. Only about five or six stores," Rose answered with a face and they both started laughing.

"Yeah, I think boys are easier when it comes to clothes," Claire said. "They don't care what they wear as long as you buy it, wash it and pick it out for them."

"Yeah, girls are not that easy going about it, but Evie is pretty laid back compared to most girls," Rose said.

"I think we should get going," Logan said, who was slightly nervous seeing his mom and Evie's mom talking so much. He was just waiting for something embarrassing to come out.

"Before you go, do you two need any tips on how to dance?" Logan's dad asked. "I can show you some moves," he said as he started to dance. *There it is*, Logan thought.

"Oh no, Dad, please stop! Okay, now we really need to go," Logan said.

Rose and Noah drove Evie and Logan to the dance and Logan thought it was weird that they walked into the school with them too. He also noticed them looking around quite a bit and thoroughly checking the place out. Evie had to tell her parents to go once they walked them all the way into the cafeteria where the dance was located.

"You can go now," Evie said to her parents. "I will see you in a few hours, Dad."

"Your parents are picking you up from here, right Logan?" Noah asked.

"Yes, they are," Logan confirmed.

"And I can expect you to be a perfect gentleman to my daughter tonight, right?" Noah asked Logan much to Evie's embarrassment.

"Of course, I…" Logan was starting to say when Evie interrupted.

"Oh my gosh, Dad, stop! Haven't you guys embarrassed me enough already? Really, it's time to go," Evie said to both of her parents.

"Well, have fun you two," Rose said and she and Noah anxiously left their daughter.

"So," Logan said to Evie as they were finally alone, "how are you?"

"Good," said Evie, even though she was a little uncomfortable in her dress and even more so in the shoes she was wearing. "How are you?"

"Great," said Logan, who really meant it. "You look really pretty."

"Oh, thank you," Evie said and she could feel her cheeks turning red. "You look nice too. I like your blue tie. It's my favorite color," she said as she motioned towards her dress. "I've never seen you in a tie before."

"Yeah, I never really wear them," Logan replied. "Maybe once or twice to a wedding or something."

"Yeah, I never wear dresses or shoes like this either," said

Evie as she fidgeted around.

"Well, they both look really nice," said Logan who was trying to think of something to talk about.

"Thanks," said Evie who suddenly also had nothing to say.

"You should wear dresses more often, they really suit you," Logan said.

"I wouldn't count on it," Evie said with a smile. Logan smiled too and they both became silent. They usually didn't have any trouble having things to talk about, but this situation was unusual. Evie started feeling really self-conscious. Thankfully, Kat and Rion both walked in at that moment and came over to Evie and Logan.

"Hey, guys," Rion said. "Doesn't everyone look nice?" he said with a sarcastic tone.

"Hey," Evie said to Rion and Kat. "You guys look great too. I like your dress," Evie said to Kat.

"Yeah, I like yours too," Kat said to Evie. "I can't believe you're wearing a dress. And those shoes! Wow. She must really like you, Logan, to wear all of this."

"Kat!" Evie exclaimed and gave a fierce look to her friend. Evie did notice that Logan smiled pretty big at this though.

Just then a new song came on and Kat suddenly called out, "I love this song! Let's all go dance!" She grabbed Evie and Rion by the hand and started pulling them out to the dance floor. Evie didn't want Logan to be left out so she reached out and grabbed Logan's hand. She wasn't sure about this but she did it anyway. Logan held Evie's hand back and gave it a little squeeze. This made Evie feel better and they walked onto the dance floor holding hands.

The song that was playing was a fast song so they all danced together as a group. They formed a little circle and put their best moves on display. Evie was a pretty good dancer but she was a little shy about her dancing. Kat was not shy about her dancing and she was really getting into it. Rion and Logan were both barely dancing but just moving around a little and mostly watching the girls. They were all having a blast though. They all stayed on the dance floor for three more fast songs and were dancing and laughing through them all.

After the fourth song in a row, Logan asked Evie if she wanted to go get something to drink. She was getting thirsty, so she left the dance floor with him. Kat and Rion went with them too. They were all standing around drinking punch and talking when the first slow song of the night came on. Logan set down his drink and started fidgeting with his hands. He seemed nervous all of a sudden. Evie looked over at him and asked, "Everything okay?"

"Yeah," Logan responded. "I was just wondering, would like to dance with me to this song?"

Evie suddenly realized that it was a slow song that was playing. She thought about chickening out but she knew that she wanted to dance with Logan. "Yes," she answered. This time Logan grabbed Evie by the hand and they walked out onto the dance floor. Evie felt so nervous. She had never danced with anyone before but she had seen it on television and in movies, so she just put her hands on Logan's shoulders and around his neck and he put his arms at her waist and they swayed back and forth. At first, Evie thought the song was lasting forever, but when it was over, it felt like it went by so fast.

They walked back over to Kat and Rion who had stayed off the dance floor for the slow song. The music was back to being a fast song and they all decided to go back to dancing together. The night was so much fun and it was going by so fast. For most of the night, they danced as a group to fast songs. This worked well for Rion who was too nervous to ask Kat if she wanted to dance to a slow song, especially since they were there officially as friends.

At one point, Evie needed to use the restroom and remembered that she was supposed to take someone with her, so she asked Kat if she would go too. Evie hated to be so cliché, girls going to the bathroom together, but she knew it was necessary. Kat agreed and they left the guys for a few minutes. When they got back, Rion walked quickly over to Evie and pulled her aside.

"Oh man, Evie, I know you don't wear dresses very much, so I think you made a mistake," Rion said. "Your dress is tucked in, in the back and your underwear is showing."

"What?" Evie exclaimed and whipped her head around to check her dress and pull it down. That's when she realized that Rion was messing with her and her dress was perfectly fine and her underwear was not showing. "I am so going to smack you, Orion," she said as she hit Rion in the shoulder. Rion was just laughing and really proud of himself.

"What is so funny?" Kat asked Rion as she didn't hear what he said to Evie.

"Oh, I just really got Evie good," Rion replied.

As Rion told Kat how he tricked Evie, which Kat couldn't help but to think was funny, Evie noticed Logan was standing with a few other friends so she thought she may have a few moments to plan something with Kat. She whispered to Kat, "Get Rion to go and get you something to drink."

"Hey, Rion, could you get me something to drink?" Kat asked.

"Shhure," Rion said as he eyed Kat and Evie, knowing they

were up to something.

Evie told Kat she wanted to get back at Rion and asked if she had any ideas. As they stood there together trying to think of something, Logan walked up.

"Hey guys, what's going on?" he asked.

Evie didn't want to tell Logan about the prank Rion pulled on her, so she gave a look to Kat trying to tell her that. Kat seemed to get Evie's point. Evie also didn't want to leave Logan out, so she tried to include him.

"We're trying to think of a prank to pull on Rion," Evie said. "He's always getting me and I want to get him back. Any ideas?"

As they all stood there thinking, suddenly the perfect idea came to Evie.

"I've got it!" Evie exclaimed.

"What is it?" Kat asked.

"I don't have time to tell you, just distract Rion for me for a little bit, okay?"

"No problem," Kat replied just as Rion walked back up to them. Kat did her best to distract Rion by pulling him back on the dance floor.

Evie told Logan to come with her and they made their way over to the DJ. Evie quickly had a conversation with the DJ and then she and Logan joined Kat and Rion on the dance floor before Rion noticed anything.

They were all dancing together when the song ended and the DJ came over the microphone.

"Hey, everybody," the DJ said, "I've never had a request for this song before and I'm surprised I could even find it, but apparently it is very important to one of you to hear it. So, for Rion Wilton, here is 'The Hokey Pokey!'"

As the kids' song started playing, everyone looked at Rion

and started laughing. Rion turned a little red, but mostly just took it and waved to the crowd. Evie, Kat and Logan were all cracking up. Rion had to admit that Evie got him really good and he started laughing too. Then they all proceeded to the dance floor to do The Hokey Pokey, which would have been really embarrassing if most of the school wasn't already doing it. After this, they danced to a few more fast songs.

It was almost the end of the dance and the DJ played another slow song. They were all still standing on the dance floor this time when it came on and Logan just held out his hand to Evie and they started dancing together. Kat and Rion still had not danced to a slow song together. They both kind of looked around and fidgeted a little when Kat suddenly grew bold. She looked at Rion and said, "Well, are you going to ask me to dance or what?"

"Yeah," Rion replied.

"Well, ask me then," Kat said smiling.

"Would you like to dance with me?" Rion asked.

"Yes, I would," Kat said and she and Rion started dancing too. Neither of them had ever slow danced before either and they just copied what Evie and Logan were doing.

Evie was having such a good time and she didn't want the night to end. She thought it was going perfect and nothing could make it better. As she and Logan were dancing, she noticed that it seemed like Logan wanted to say something. She thought that if she said something, it might get him talking.

"I'm having a great time," Evie said. "Are you having fun?"

"Yeah, I'm having a great time too," Logan responded.

"I'm glad you asked me to come," Evie said still trying to get Logan talking.

"Me too," Logan said nervously. "Um, there was something else I wanted to ask you."

"Oh, okay," Evie said. She could tell this was what he had been waiting to say and she looked forward to hearing what it was going to be.

"Well, I was just wondering," Logan said slowly, "would you, um, would you want to go out with me?"

"Sure," Evie said, "but go out where?"

"No," Logan kind of smiled, "I mean, would you, you know, um, be my girlfriend?"

"Oh," said Evie. This surprised her but she managed to put her thoughts together quickly. Thankfully, she knew the answer she wanted to give right away. "Yes," Evie replied. She didn't know what to say now and things suddenly seemed a little awkward. She wanted to make things seem normal, so she added, "thank you." She and Logan both found this funny and they both started laughing. It was the perfect thing to take the awkwardness away. They just continued dancing and Evie had never felt so happy.

The dance was over shortly after this and Evie's dad had walked into the school to pick her up. Once again, Logan thought it was weird that he came inside as his parents were waiting outside to pick him up. Evie, Logan, Kat and Rion all said their goodbyes to each other. Evie said to Kat and Rion that she would text them later as she wanted to tell them about her news.

Evie and her dad were on their way home. Evie was on cloud nine. She was so happy that she felt like she was floating. It had been the perfect night. Her dad was asking her all about the dance.

"Did you have a good time?" Noah asked.

"Yes, I did," Evie replied and she was grinning from ear to ear, which her dad couldn't help but notice and he wanted to know what that was about.

"Did anything strange or out of the ordinary happen?" Noah continued with his questions.

"Nope, everything was super normal," Evie replied but Noah knew something had happened.

"So, nothing happened that would be news worthy?" Noah asked still trying to figure out what Evie's huge smile was about. Evie was thinking about how Logan asked her to be his girlfriend as this was definitely news worthy, but she didn't want to tell her dad about this, so she thought of something else to say.

"Well, I pranked Rion and it went great. He turned so red. I was loving it," Evie answered.

"Oh, that sounds good, what'd you do?" her dad asked.

"I got the DJ to play 'The Hokey Pokey' and say that Rion requested it. The whole school thought Rion asked to hear it. It was hilarious."

"That sounds hilarious," Noah replied. "Good one, honey. Hey, did I ever tell you that I used to be addicted to 'The Hokey Pokey?'"

"Dad, what are you talking about?" Evie asked, sensing a dad joke coming on.

"Yeah," Noah replied, "I was addicted to 'The Hokey Pokey' but then I turned myself around."

"Dad, you're such a nerd," Evie said, but she couldn't help but laugh.

She was laughing and talking with her dad as they were proceeding through an intersection. WHAM! Suddenly a truck ran the red light and slammed into Evie and Noah's car on Evie's side. The truck had been going fast and hit their car really hard. Noah and Evie were both unconscious. The car was totaled.

CHAPTER 9

THE HOSPITAL & THE REVEAL

Noah woke up to a chaotic scene. There were sirens going off and red and blue lights everywhere. He could hear people talking and a voice close to him was saying something about remaining still and they were working to get him out of the car. He suddenly thought of Evie and whipped his head to the right to check on his daughter. The man outside the car yelled to him to try to stay still. Evie was still unconscious but somehow she was still aware of her surroundings.

"Evie, sweetie," Noah yelled. "Are you okay? Wake up honey!" Evie heard her father say this but she couldn't answer.

Evie couldn't move but she could hear everything that was going on around her. She heard the paramedics get Noah out of the car and put him on a gurney quickly. She knew they were having more trouble with getting her out, as the car was really smashed in on her side. Evie heard her dad asking the paramedics about her. They kept telling him that they were working on getting her out but that it was taking longer because of the condition of the car and because they were being particularly careful in case there were any spinal injuries.

"I need to call my wife," Evie heard Noah say.

"We'll call her for you. Don't worry," the paramedics responded.

"Who hit us?" Noah asked the people around him.

"We don't know, sir," one policeman replied. "The driver of the other car fled the scene in the car, so both the driver and the car are currently missing."

"It was a truck," Noah told the man. Evie was glad that her dad had noticed this too as she couldn't tell them.

"That is good to know," said the policeman. "We'll be looking for him or her and the truck. Try not to worry."

Evie felt the firemen and paramedics get her out of the car but she was still unconscious. She had some cuts and bruises on her face and body, but there wasn't any major bleeding otherwise. The paramedics wanted to get her to the hospital as soon as possible in case there was any internal bleeding. Noah had already left in an ambulance for the hospital and now Evie was on her way too.

Evie and Noah both underwent many X-rays, scans and tests at the hospital. Noah seemed to be okay, other than some pretty bad cuts and bruises. He needed some stitches for some of the deep cuts. Evie, though, was not okay. Though she was still aware of everything, she had remained unconscious. The doctors suspected she had some internal bleeding and damage so they informed Noah that she would need surgery and they were taking her there very soon. She was breathing on her own, which was a very good thing.

After a while, Rose arrived at the hospital and found Noah. She caught them just before they took Evie back to surgery.

"How is Evie?" Rose asked and Evie heard this.

"I'm not sure, they're not really telling me anything," Noah replied with frustration. "She's going to surgery soon and they said she had a broken arm and leg. Both on the side the truck hit. There could be more damage, though, internally."

"I can't believe this," Rose said as she started crying. "It must be the same guy again. I never thought he would go this far. Please, God, let her be okay."

I'm okay, Mom and Dad, don't worry, Evie thought as the nurses came and took her away for surgery.

Evie felt like she was in surgery for forever and she knew her parents must feel the same way. She could hear the doctors talking as they worked on her. Then suddenly there was a beeping noise and Evie heard a doctor say that she had stopped breathing. Evie did feel different and then she finally lost awareness of the world.

She became aware of her surroundings again a little while later but she was still unconscious. She must have been wheeled into a room with her parents again because she could hear them talking.

"Why does she have that tube down her throat?" Evie heard her mom ask with worry in her voice.

"I'm not sure," replied Noah. "Hopefully, the doctor will be here soon to give us an update."

Evie heard Cy and Rion arrive at the hospital to help in any way they could. There wasn't much for them to do though. After what seemed like a very long time, Evie heard a doctor finally come out to talk to Noah and Rose.

"How is she?" Evie heard her parents ask together.

"The surgery went great," the doctor informed them. "We immediately started working on the internal bleeding but we found some damage to her intestines too. The internal bleeding has been stopped but the intestinal damage will take some more time to heal and possibly more surgeries in the future. We also worked on her broken arm and leg, both of which required some metal pins and screws to keep them in place. There is some bad news that I am sorry to report," the doctor continued. "Evie stopped breathing on her own and we had to hook her up to machines to breathe for her. She is now on life support."

"Oh no," Rose cried. "Please do whatever it takes to help her. Please keep her alive." Rose started crying and Noah grabbed his wife and held her in his arms. Evie hated that she couldn't tell her parents that she was okay.

"She'll be fine," Noah said trying to console his wife. But he was worried too and scared and suddenly very angry.

"Thank you, doctor," Noah said trying to ignore his anger. He continued to hold his sobbing wife for a while and held back his own tears. "I need to find the police," he said as he could not ignore his anger any longer. "I need to find out if they found who was driving that truck."

Noah stood up and Cy stopped him. "You were in the accident too, Noah, you should rest," Evie heard Cy say to Noah. "Let me help. I will look around the hospital for the police officers who were at the scene. We will find this guy."

"Thanks, Cy," Noah said.

Rose and Noah went back to waiting as Cy and Rion went to look for the police officers. They came back to Evie's room with some information.

"We found a police officer at the front of the building and asked him if he knew anything," Cy told Rose and Noah and though he didn't know it, he told Evie too. "He said he would make some calls." Everyone went back to waiting together for what seemed like a very long time when a police officer finally came to Evie's room to talk to them.

"Hello, I am looking for the people who were in the accident tonight, the hit and run," the officer said. "The nurse said I would find you all here."

"Yes," Noah replied, "that was me and my daughter. She's

still unconscious, unfortunately. We were driving through a green light when a truck ran the red light and hit us on my daughter's side."

"Yes, he or she did," the officer said. "We are still not sure of who was driving the truck; if it was a man or a woman."

"It was a man," Noah said. "I know it's the same guy we called you about that tried to attack our daughter at the school. He's trying to kill our daughter!" Noah almost yelled.

"Please, sir, try to stay calm," Evie heard the officer said. "We are aware that someone tried to attack your daughter before and we are keeping that in mind. For now, what we know is that whoever was driving the truck had stolen the vehicle. Then he drove it a little ways away from the scene of the accident and abandoned it on foot. So, whoever was driving has gotten away for now. So far, we haven't found any evidence and since he stole the truck, there is no record of him. We are looking for the person though and we have the hospital on alert to report any person who comes in with injuries typically associated with a front-end collision. Is there anything else you can tell us about the accident? Do you remember anything about the driver of the truck?"

"I didn't see him very well," Noah replied. "I wish there was more that I could tell you. I was unconscious after he hit us, so I didn't see him drive away."

"That's okay," the officer said. "We are checking cameras to see if there are any pictures of him and we are checking the red-light camera. That should show us something."

"Thank you so much for all you're doing," Rose said. "Just out of curiosity, what will happen to the guy if you find him?"

"He will be charged with theft of a vehicle and a hit and run," the officer replied. "If the worst happens, he will be charged with manslaughter."

"Oh no, Evie will be fine. She is going to be fine," Rose responded. "Please don't even say that." Evie heard her mom start to cry again.

"Don't get upset, Rose," Cy said to his sister. "She is going to be fine."

"Yes, she is," Noah added as he held his wife. "And he should be charged with attempted homicide, as he did this on purpose," Noah said to the officer.

"I'm sorry, I didn't mean to upset you," the officer said. "Here is a number where you can reach me if you have any more questions or if you think of anything else that might be helpful. I will be in touch if we find out anything new."

"Thank you, officer," Cy said.

Evie was aware that the doctor came back just a little while after the police officer left. He had come back to see if Noah and Rose had any questions.

"Okay," Rose said. "I don't even know where to begin. How long do you think she will be on life support? Is she in pain? Did she wake up at all?"

"Since she has remained unconscious, she is not in any pain," said the doctor. "There is no way to know how long she will be on life support and no, she did not wake up at all during her surgery." After seeing their faces look discouraged, he added, "I feel like she will be okay. As I said, the surgery went really well and she is young and strong." Evie was glad to hear this.

"Okay, thank you doctor," Rose said as Noah shook his hand.

By now, it was the next morning and they all continued waiting for Evie to wake up. Rose and Noah just stared at their daughter. It was so scary seeing her hooked up to the breathing machine and to all the IV's. She looked so small in that big hospital bed. They felt so helpless. Everyone wished there was something they could do. Rose and Noah could not be talked into leaving the hospital all day, not even for a little bit. They just sat and waited all day with no changes. Cy and Rion left for a little while, but they planned on coming back very soon. When they did come back, they tried to convince Rose and Noah to go home for a bit to shower and get some clean clothes. When they couldn't convince them of that, Cy insisted that they go to the cafeteria to get something to eat as they hadn't eaten all day and it was evening now. It took a while but Cy finally convinced them to do this. Evie was glad that her uncle had convinced her parents to go and eat. She felt bad that they had been with her all day and she couldn't even talk to them.

Cy and Rion sat with Evie while her parents were gone. Rion was thirsty so his dad gave him some money to go to the vending machines. Cy was the only one still with Evie when Evie heard him get up and go to the bathroom. He hesitated to go, but decided it would be fine since there was a bathroom right there in Evie's room. What he didn't know was that the guy trying to kill Evie was watching and waiting for a time when Evie was alone. The killer knew he needed to act quickly. As soon as Cy closed the door behind him, Evie heard the killer walk into her room. He looked around for a way to finish the job. He knew he wouldn't have many more chances. He noticed that Evie was hooked up to machines so he grabbed the cords to Evie's life support and unplugged them. There was one monitor that he didn't unplug and it started beeping which alerted both the hospital staff and Cy. Cy was washing his hands when he heard it. He ran out of the bathroom just in time to see the guy starting to run away. Cy lunged after him and tackled him just outside Evie's door. They almost blocked the door that the doctors and nurses were rushing through to check on Evie. Evie could hear Cy and the killer wrestling on the floor and Cy was having trouble holding him. He was scared he was going to get away from him. Just as Cy was about to lose his grip, Rion came around the corner and Cy yelled to him, "Help me, I've got him! Help me hold him!" Rion ran over to his dad and helped him hold down the killer.

"Call the police, call 911," Cy yelled to Rion now that he had a better grip on the killer. Rion grabbed his phone and called 911. He told the police that he was at the hospital and that someone had just tried to kill his cousin and that his dad was holding him. They had a car close by and the police were on their way. Cy just had to hold the guy a little while longer. He wasn't going to get away.

Cy wanted to know who this guy was so he wrestled him around and pulled the hoodie off his head to see his face. Rion didn't recognize him because he had never met him before. But Cy knew the guy looked familiar, but couldn't quite place who he was.

"Get off me," the killer yelled. "Let me go!"

Cy and Rion didn't know who this guy was, but Evie recognized his voice. She could barely believe her ears, because she swore that sounded just like Logan's older brother, Carter!

CHAPTER 10

THE KILLER & THE UNCERTAINTY

The doctors and nurses who rushed in to check on Evie quickly discovered what the problem was and plugged in her machines right away. With their quick response, Evie was fine and there was no harm done. She was still not awake or breathing on her own, though. She still needed the machines.

Evie could hear that Cy and Rion successfully held on to Carter until the police arrived. The police took him into custody and took him to the station to question him. A few hours later a police officer called Noah and updated him. After Noah got off the phone, he shared everything with Rose.

"So, the police have the suspect in custody and he matches up with the picture from the red light camera so they feel sure they have the right guy," Evie heard Noah say.

"Oh, thank goodness," Rose said. "I hope this means that Evie is safe now. Who was he? Did they tell you the suspect's name?"

"Well, yes, they did. And it's upsetting to learn, honey. Are you sure you want to know?"

"Of course I do," Rose answered. "This whole thing is upsetting."

"Okay," Noah continued. "I'm sorry to say this, but the suspect is Carter Millan, Logan's older brother."

"Evie's friend, Logan, the one she just went to the dance with?" Rose asked in disbelief.

Evie couldn't believe what she was hearing either. She thought she heard Carter's voice but she figured she must be wrong. Now, she knew she wasn't wrong.

"Yes, unfortunately, that same Logan. This is devastating."

"Now, what do we do about Logan?" Rose asked.

"Let's not worry about that now," Noah said. "He may not be a part of Evie's life anymore after this anyway."

Evie heard this and it depressed her more than learning she was on life support.

"Did Carter confess to attacking her at the school or poisoning her?" Rose asked.

"Actually, no," Noah answered. "The police said Carter has not confessed anything. They said he seems really ashamed and won't say anything. They do have evidence against him though because of the picture from the red-light camera and he was working at the restaurant where Evie was poisoned."

"Oh my gosh," Rose said. "So, he was working there when Evie was poisoned?"

"Yes, he was," Noah answered. "They think they have enough evidence to convict him even if he never confesses anything."

"This is all too unbelievable," Rose said as Evie had the exact same thought. "I'm glad that he's in custody though. I hope we can just focus on Evie getting better now. But there's still one thing bothering me. Why did he do it? What was his motive?"

"The police have no idea as the answer to that," Noah said. "They did tell me that they were going to continue to question Carter to try and find this out. Hopefully, we'll know this… one day."

A week later and nothing had changed for Evie. She was still in a coma but she could also still hear everything that was going on around her. This was a good thing because otherwise she would have been going crazy. Her parents were with her most of the time. Her mom was with her the most.

"Hi, honey, how was your day?" Rose asked when Noah joined her in Evie's hospital room that evening after work.

"It was fine, had an interesting call from the detective today," Noah replied.

"Oh yeah? Is there something new with Carter?" Rose asked.

"Yes, there is. They told me that he pleaded guilty. He is going to take a deal," Noah said. "They said he knew he would probably be found guilty since they had so much evidence against him. It will also allow him to avoid a trial and he will probably end up with a lighter sentence."

"Well, I'm not sure how I feel about that," Rose said.

"I don't like it," Noah said. "I wanted this guy to be behind bars for a long time. Then we could feel like Evie is safe."

"Now that he has pleaded guilty, did they say if he told them why he did it? What was his motive?"

"I was hoping that he confessed that too, but he didn't. The detective said Carter still won't tell them why he did it."

"Oh, it's so frustrating to not know why he did this all to our daughter!" Rose said.

The conversation Evie's parents were having was interrupted by the doctor coming in to Evie's room.

"Hello, Mr. and Mrs. Baker, how are you?"

"Fine, thank you," Rose answered. "Is there anything new with our daughter?"

"Yes, we want to plan her next surgery," the doctor answered.

"Already?" Noah asked.

"Yes, as soon as possible," the doctor said. "We want

everything to heal correctly. It will be a long road to recovery for Evie and the sooner she starts that journey, the better."

"Okay," responded Noah. "Is that the only news?"

"Actually, I did want to talk to you about one other thing," the doctor answered as his face changed. "We are concerned that Evie is still not breathing on her own. We just want you to be prepared for how things may turn out. There is a chance she will never wake up."

"No, I won't accept that," Rose said with authority. "I know Evie will wake up. It's just a matter of time."

"Well, we hope you're right," the doctor said.

Evie wasn't glad to hear this. She thought she was okay but hearing the doctor say this made her worry that she was going to be stuck like this forever. She was starting to go a little stir crazy. Thankfully, someone was with her almost all the time. Even though they had caught Carter, her family and friends were still nervous to leave her alone. They also wanted for someone to be there when she woke up. Between Noah, Rose, Cy, Rion and Kat, someone was always with her. Every day they hoped today would be the day that she would wake up. She could hear them saying these things to her. She also heard Logan try to visit her one day.

"Can I see Evie?" Evie heard Logan's voice for the first time since she had arrived at the hospital. It made her heart soar.

"Sorry, Logan, but no," Noah answered.

Evie's heart sank.

"We just don't feel like it's appropriate for you to visit Evie considering the situation with your brother," Rose told Logan.

"But I don't understand," Logan replied. "I'm not my brother. I would never hurt Evie."

"We know you wouldn't hurt Evie, or at least, we're pretty sure you wouldn't," Noah said. "But we can't take any chances and we don't want there to be any connection between your brother and Evie. We don't want anything to affect the outcome of his sentencing."

"I wouldn't do anything to shorten his sentence," Logan assured them. "I want him to be punished for what he did. I want him to be locked away too so he can't hurt or try to hurt Evie again."

"Well, I'm glad to hear that, but it doesn't change our minds," Noah said. "We don't know Carter's motive or if it involved you or your friendship with Evie."

"What do you mean?" Logan asked.

"We don't know if it involves some sort of jealousy of you or something," Rose answered.

"I really don't think it has anything to do with me," Logan said. "If anything, it probably has something to do with Carter being adopted."

"Carter's adopted?" Noah asked.

"Yeah, we both are," Logan answered. "Carter told my parents that this was why he attacked Evie; that he was hurt that his parents had given him up and he was jealous that Evie had her real parents and that they loved her so much. So, he was jealous, just not of me. But of Evie."

"So, he said that's why he attacked our daughter?" Rose asked. "We've been wondering why he did this. That doesn't sound like enough of a reason to try and kill someone. But it's nice to have an answer."

"Well, I'm glad I could answer that for you," Logan replied. "My parents were all worried about me too after Carter told them this. They thought I would become all angry and bitter like Carter about being given up by my biological parents. They were concerned that I would eventually do something crazy or act out in some way. I told them I didn't even care about my real parents. They were drug addicts who could barely take care of themselves much less me. I don't need them. Max and Claire are my real parents and they are great. They are all that I need. I have them. And I have Evie," he said as he looked at Evie. "Or at least I hope I will still have her in my life."

"I'm sorry, Logan," Noah answered. "We really appreciate you telling us all of this, but we are still not comfortable with you seeing Evie. At least, for now. Once again, I'm sorry, but you need to leave."

Evie wanted to scream. She was screaming, "No!" in her head. She wished she could talk to her parents. This really bummed Evie out. It bummed Logan out too. Logan wondered if he would ever be allowed to see Evie again.

Another week passed and Evie still hadn't woken up. No one wanted to say it out loud, but they were all starting to worry that Evie was never going to wake up. Evie wanted to tell them that she was fine but she couldn't. She just listened as her mom talked to her about some recipe or something or her dad shared about his day or Kat gave updates about the soccer team, which wasn't doing so great without Evie. It was as if they knew Evie could hear them. Even Rion would tell her jokes and she would laugh in her head. She wanted to laugh out loud. She wanted to wake up.

CHAPTER 11

EVIE'S FATE & LOGAN'S VISIT

Finally, after eighteen days since the accident, Evie opened her eyes. She was still hooked up to machines and could not talk. Her mom was there with her and she could see from Evie's facial expression that Evie was scared and wanted the tubes taken out of her throat.

"Oh, Evie! You're awake! Don't worry, sweetie, you're going to be fine," her mother told her while holding back tears. "Everything is fine. We'll get the doctor to get that tube out of your throat as soon as possible. You and your dad were in a car accident the night of the dance. Don't worry, your dad is fine. A truck hit the car on your side so you were hurt more than your father." Rose was thrilled that her daughter was awake but she tried to remain calm to keep Evie calm. But on the inside, Rose was so relieved and elated.

Just then, Rion came in with his dad and saw that Evie was awake. He was so excited.

"Evie, you're awake!" Rion said. "I can't believe it. You've been asleep for eighteen days!"

Evie's eyes got really wide when she heard this. Time had been fuzzy to Evie. She couldn't believe she had been in the hospital for so long. This seemed to upset Evie to learn she had been missing life for all this time. Evie also realized she must have been really hurt if it took her that long to wake up. Rose saw

Evie's face and didn't want to upset her while she was still recovering. This made Rose wonder how much she or anyone should tell Evie. She decided to wait until Evie was stronger to tell her about Carter.

"Let's not upset Evie, Rion. We can tell her more after she recovers," Rose said giving Cy and Rion a look. Cy and Rion picked up on Rose's look and knew not to say anything more about the accident. "You two stay with her while I go and get the doctor."

Evie started doing much better straight away and she was unhooked from the breathing machine that was helping her. She could finally breathe on her own again. It took another day for her to be able to talk and even then, she had to limit her talking as her throat was very sore and she was still weak. Over the next few days though, she was recovering nicely and getting her strength back. She was happiest when she had a visitor which was most of the time. Once again, her mom was there almost all the time and her dad was there when he wasn't at work. Cy and Rion were there regularly and Kat visited often too. She even had some other friends from her soccer team visit. All of this was a great distraction from the pain and the boredom. But one thing was really bothering her. She kept waiting for Logan to try and visit again but he never came. It was really starting to upset her. Her memory from her time in the coma was hazy. She didn't remember much from the time after she left the dance, but she did remember most of the dance and she definitely remembered that Logan had asked her to be his girlfriend. *How could he not visit again?* she wondered. Even though her parents had asked him to leave, she still thought he would try again. He hadn't even texted her and she didn't know whether she should text him or not. She was feeling insecure about the whole situation. She finally told Kat and Rion about Logan asking her to be his girlfriend as she had never had the chance to tell them after the dance. She told them she couldn't understand why he hadn't been there to visit since she woke up and she noticed their faces get weird. She could tell there was something they weren't telling her. They didn't know that Evie had heard Logan visit the one time or that Evie already knew about Carter as Evie hadn't told anyone that she could hear them when she was unconscious.

"What is going on guys?" Evie asked them. "Every time that I bring up Logan, you guys get weird looks on your faces. Is there something that I need to know?" Evie suddenly became worried that Logan had decided he didn't like her anymore and had a new girl he liked. "Does he like someone else or something?"

"No, it's not that at all," Kat said. "He's been really worried about you. He asks me about you every day. He can't wait to see you again. He misses you. He was so happy to hear that you woke up."

"Then why isn't he visiting me here?" Evie asked. "It doesn't make sense. If he misses me, then he should visit."

"Well, he tried to," Kat started to say and Rion stopped her.

"No, Kat. Not now," Rion said.

"Yeah," Evie said as she sat up more in bed and winced at the pain. "I sorta know. Look, I haven't said anything but I could kind of hear everything when I was unconscious. I heard him visit and I heard mom and dad tell him to leave. Is that why he hasn't tried to visit again? Because of my parents? Or is something else going on?"

"You need to ask your parents, Evie," Rion said not wanting to be the one who told Evie about Carter. "It's not our place to tell you. Let's go, Kat, so she can talk to her parents."

Evie's parents walked into Evie's room after Kat and Rion

left. Rion had told them that she was asking questions about Logan and that she knew something was going on. They felt it was probably time to tell her the truth. They just hoped she was strong enough. Evie started asking questions the moment they walked into the room.

"What is going on?" Evie asked. "I know there's something that you guys aren't telling me and apparently it involves Logan. Why hasn't he visited me?"

"Well, he tried to," Rose said. "And we stopped him."

"Yes, I know," Evie cried out. "Why would you stop him? That doesn't make any sense. Seriously, you guys make me so mad!"

"Evie, stay calm, you're still recovering," Noah said. "This is why we haven't told you any of this. We don't want you to get upset. It could jeopardize your health. We can only tell you everything if you stay calm."

"Okay," said Evie though she was still agitated. "I promise to stay calm. Just tell me what is going on."

"Well, the reason we sent Logan away when he came to visit is because," Noah started but he wasn't sure where to begin, "well, we found out who was trying to kill you and he is someone close to Logan."

"It was Carter," Evie blurted out.

"Who told you?" Rose asked. "I told Rion not to say anything. I didn't want to upset you."

"Rion didn't tell me anything," Evie said. "I heard it all happen. I heard him come here and I heard you guys talking about it. I heard it all while I was unconscious." Evie's parents couldn't believe this.

"You could hear everything while you were in your coma?" Noah asked. "That is crazy."

"It was crazy… and frustrating… and interesting," Evie said. "I know it sounds unbelievable but it's true. It was weird. But I'm glad I could hear everything. Now I know everything that happened. But anyways, back to Logan. I still don't understand why you stopped him from visiting me."

"Well, at some point I want to talk more about you being able to hear while you were in your coma. But for now, we need to tell you more about Carter. You probably know but Carter is adopted," Noah started. "Max and Claire are not his biological parents. But they visited us and said that he was just angry and bitter about his birth mom giving him up and he was jealous of you having your parents. At least that is all they told us. But Cy did some investigating and he discovered that Carter found his birth mother and she told him that he was an elf, like you. Carter and his mom are both elves and Cy found out this is true. We're still not exactly sure why Carter was trying to kill you so we're continuing to guess that it may be because he knows you're an elf and the last elf girl and he wanted to end the elf people. We don't understand why he would want to end his own people, but that is all we have to go on for now. He never told his parents or the police about anyone being an elf so no one knows about that."

"Evie?" Rose said as Evie wasn't saying anything.

"I still can't believe Carter tried to kill me," Evie said as she had never really let that sink in. "He seemed so normal when I met him. At least, nothing like a killer."

"His parents are shocked. They can't believe he would've done anything like this. They say he was a normal kid before all of this. Sometimes it's too easy for a person to be convinced of something when they are in pain or feel that they've been wronged. For some reason, Carter convinced himself that killing you would make him feel better."

"So, Carter's an elf too?"

"Yes, he is," Rose replied.

"Do you know if Logan is too?" Evie was hoping Logan was an elf too.

"No, we don't think Logan is an elf too. He and Carter have different biological parents," Rose told her.

"So, Logan's adopted too? I thought I heard him say that."

"Yes, Evie, Logan is adopted too."

"But wait, I still don't understand why you sent Logan away when he tried to visit me?" Evie asked. "He had nothing to do with it. He's not his brother."

"Honey, we didn't feel it was a good idea for Logan to be here considering his brother was trying to kill you," Noah said. "The circumstances are extreme."

"But that's not fair," Evie replied. "I understand these are extreme circumstances and that it's totally crazy that Carter turned out to be the killer but Carter isn't Logan! Logan, I'm sure, didn't even know about Carter. He's probably in just as much shock as we are, if not more. I want to see Logan! It's not like I will be in any danger to see him, so what's the difference? What is the problem, really?"

"Look, we understand your point of view," Rose said, "and we get it that it frustrates you that we would keep you from seeing Logan. But at first, when he tried to visit, we didn't have all the information that we have now. I guess maybe, now that things are a little more settled, we could let you see Logan."

"I'm not so sure," Noah added. "I mean, he's just a friend and a new friend. You're not even that close to him, are you?"

"Well," Evie started. "Yeah, I am close to him. He's a really good friend now and well… at the dance, he sort of asked me… to uh, be his girlfriend."

"Oh, you're his girlfriend?" Rose asked in a sweet tone.

"Uh, yeah," Evie bashfully replied.

"I don't think I like that," Noah added.

"Oh, come on, Noah, you know you had a girlfriend when you were her age. Or at least, your friends did," Rose said ribbing Noah.

"Well, yes, that's true, *I* did," Noah said. "But I still don't like it."

"Dad?" Evie asked, and her dad knew she was asking to see Logan and that this was very important to her.

"Okay, we'll let Logan come visit you," Noah replied. "But we need to be here in the hospital. We can go to the cafeteria or something."

"Thank you, thank you, thank you!" Evie exclaimed. "Can you hand me my phone, I want to text him to tell him."

Logan was so happy to get Evie's text. He was so upset when her parents had told him he couldn't visit and he had been hoping to get a text from her ever since he heard she was awake. He planned on visiting her right away.

Evie was a little embarrassed for Logan to see her in her hospital bed, but she did her best to look nice. She had her mom help her wash and brush her hair. Logan arrived with a bouquet of flowers.

"These are for you, I hope you're feeling better," Logan said nervously.

"Oh, thank you, they're beautiful," Evie said nervously too. "I love them. Can you put them on the table for me?"

"Sure," Logan said. "So, how're you feeling?"

"Not that bad, really. I mean, I do have some pain, but the worst part is that I have to stay in this bed all the time. It is so boring. And now I am just starting to get some homework from school, you know, so I don't get too far behind while I'm in here, so that sucks. Having visitors is the best part. I'm really glad you're here."

"I'm really glad to be here. I kept hoping to hear from you. I missed you," Logan said and he immediately started blushing. He tried to recover, "I mean, school isn't the same without you there. Like, school is never really fun, but it was always better with you being there."

"Yeah, I would miss you too if I was at school without you," Evie said, trying to make Logan feel less nervous.

"Look, Evie," Logan started, "I had no idea about Carter. My entire family was so shocked by this. Carter was such a normal kid and had been a normal guy all his life until just a little while ago. Something had changed with him. He wasn't like crazy or anything, but he did seem a little different lately. But I still would never have thought in a million years, that he would do something like this."

"It's just so crazy," Evie said. "He seemed so nice when I met him. I mean, he was kind of picking on us and stuff, but he seemed like a normal big brother."

"Yeah, it is crazy," Logan said. "He was like a normal big brother. But now, I think he regrets what he did. I think he realizes that he went too far. I'm hopeful that things are different again now. I don't think he will be a danger to you anymore."

"Well, I really hope not," Evie replied. "I hope something makes him feel differently about me."

"I've been trying to talk to him about you," Logan said. "I've been telling him how great you are and that he shouldn't be jealous of you for having your biological parents or whatever. I think things will be different."

"Well, time will tell," Evie said. "I don't blame you for

anything. I know you didn't know anything about it."

"Oh man, I absolutely didn't know anything about it. I just wanted to bring it up though. I just felt like I had to say something," Logan said. "What is that saying? It's the elephant in the room or something."

"Yeah, I think that's the saying," Evie said. "But we don't have to talk about it. In fact, I'd rather not. Let's talk about something else."

"Sounds good to me," Logan said.

"I never got to tell you that I had so much fun at the dance," Evie said.

"Yeah, me too, that was the best night," Logan said. "Well, except for the accident, of course."

"Yeah, other than that," Evie said laughing, "it was the best night." She wanted to bring up being his girlfriend to see if that was still true, but she was too nervous to do so. "It was a really great night."

"Do you remember the whole night?" Logan asked. Logan too wanted to confirm that Evie was his girlfriend.

"I remember the entire dance," Evie said. "I don't remember everything after leaving the dance."

"But you remember the dance, though?" Logan asked. "And everything that happened?"

"Yeah," Evie said. "I had so much fun. I didn't know I would like dancing so much. And there were other parts that were great too."

"I was especially happy that you said you would be my girlfriend," Logan said as decided to just go for it and make sure that she did remember this.

"Me too," Evie said. "That was my favorite part of the night." Evie and Logan were both relieved that it had been acknowledged that they were girlfriend and boyfriend.

"Mine too," Logan said as he reached out and grabbed Evie's hand.

Evie and Logan talked and held hands for almost a couple of hours. Evie may have been lying in a hospital bed, but with Logan there, she wasn't in any pain and she had never felt happier.

CHAPTER 12

THE IDEA & FIRST VISIT

When Evie finally got out of the hospital, she was elated. It had been so boring and tedious to be in there. She was even happy to go back to school though it wasn't easy being back, with her arm and leg still in a cast, but she managed. She missed playing soccer the most. She still went to the games, to watch and give support to her teammates and especially Kat. She and Logan were very happy and hanging out regularly, even with the awkwardness of seeing Logan's parents again, being that they were also Carter's parents. Things were going pretty well, all things considered.

But something was off. Evie's anxiety had become worse. Even with the knowledge of Carter being in prison, she still felt afraid. No matter how much she would try to talk to herself and calm herself by thinking, *He's in prison, he can't hurt you, nothing bad is going to happen now*, she couldn't shake the anxiety. She couldn't stop the nightmares. She confided this to her parents.

"Do you feel up to seeing Mr. Dancy again?" Rose asked after hearing about this.

"Yeah, I think I do, I think I have to," Evie answered. "I hate feeling this way."

"I'll make an appointment for you then," Rose said. "I'm sure he will get you in right away."

And that he did. Evie went back to see him just one day later.

Once again, she had to get up extra early before school to go.

"So nice to see you again, Evie," Mr. Dancy said. "I'm so glad you are okay and on the mend."

"Thank you," Evie said. "It's nice to see you too. I'm just having trouble again. You know, with the anxiety."

"Okay, let's talk about that. Is it worse than before?"

"Yes, it is," Evie replied. "Which is weird, I think, because now I know that I'm safe and I know that Carter was the killer and he's away but I still can't let go of this fear. Why would I still be afraid?"

"It's quite normal to still feel afraid," Mr. Dancy replied. "When you have been through something so traumatic, it's going to make an impact on the brain. It's going to change how you see the world and how you react to things. Think of a soldier. They still have fear and anxiety after leaving a war zone. They are home and know they are safe now, but they still feel the same feelings as when they were in a dangerous place. They suffer from post-traumatic stress disorder and I think you are suffering from that too. Research and tests have shown that going through something traumatic can actually change a person's brain. It's not surprising at all that you feel this way."

"Well, that makes me feel better already," Evie said, "just knowing that it's normal that I feel this way. I never even thought of a soldier. I totally understand that they still feel afraid when they get home, so I guess I can understand for myself and how I feel. Thanks for that."

"Of course," Mr. Dancy said. "There are some things to do to alleviate the way you are feeling. I don't think we should move on to medications just yet. I would rather try some alternative things first. There are different therapy techniques that we can do and I think you should sign up for a yoga class. Yoga can be great in dealing with PTSD and anxiety. At our next session, we can also try to do a therapy technique known as EMDR, which stands for eye movement desensitization and reprocessing. EMDR can also be a great tool to help with PTSD. It is a technique where I will move my fingers back and forth in front of your face and you will follow my finger with your eyes while you also recall the traumatic events that have occurred. Then we will move on to more enjoyable thoughts and memories. The hope is that this will change the neural networks in your brain by connecting your traumatic memories with more pleasant ones. We will try this next time if it's okay with you and your parents."

"That sounds good to me," Evie said.

"Okay, good. For today, I want you to just talk about whatever comes to mind. I want you to tell me what's going on in your life, the good and the bad and just talk freely."

So, Evie talked and talked. She told him about going back to school, which was both good and bad, and getting used to having casts on her arm and leg. She talked about soccer and a little about Logan, which she was slightly shy about so she kept that minimal. Finally, her sharing worked its way to Carter and how the thought of him getting out of prison made her nervous. She wondered if he would come after her again. She was having nightmares that he escaped from prison.

"I'm just scared that he will be released or something and try to kill me again," Evie said. "I know that he took a deal and he will probably get a lighter sentence since he did that, so what if he's out soon? Logan says that Carter really regrets what he did now because he doesn't want to ever go back to jail. He says that Carter just wants to get back to his normal life and be the person he was before all this started. I don't know what to think. I wish there was something I could do. I feel so helpless."

"Maybe there is something you can do," Mr. Dancy said. "Do you remember when you told me you wished you knew who this person was, who was trying to kill you, so you could talk to him and try to change his mind about you. You wished you could do something to change how he feels. Well, perhaps, you could."

"What do you mean?"

"I think it may be a good idea for you to go and visit Carter; at the prison. Not only would you see for yourself that he is locked away where he can't hurt you, which may in turn alleviate your anxiety, but you could also talk with him. Try to convince him that you don't deserve to be hurt. Try to change his mind about you. I know this is a bit extreme but I think it could really help. I will talk to your parents about it if that is okay with you."

"I'm not sure," Evie said as she thought about it. It sounded scary to her. She couldn't imagine coming face to face with Carter. But she knew she wanted to do anything to help her get over this fear. *It actually might help to see him locked away*, she thought. *But I doubt I will be able to convince him to think differently about killing me. Maybe I should try.* "I guess we can see what my parents think about it."

"Sounds good, your mom is already waiting for you, so let's see what she thinks," Mr. Dancy said.

Mr. Dancy made a strong case to Rose about Evie going to see Carter. Rose wasn't sure at first, so he continued to argue for it.

"It may be the best tool we have to combat Evie's anxiety," he said, "and it may be the best chance to keep Evie safe going forward."

"Let me think on it," Rose said to Evan.

And that she did. Eventually, his argument convinced Rose, especially since she mostly wanted Evie's anxiety to get better.

But then Rose had to convince Noah, which wasn't easy. And by this time, Evie had been thinking about it too. She now thought it would be the best way to make her feel better. She not only decided she wanted to visit Carter, she was absolutely determined to do so. Together, Evie and Rose talked to Noah about it.

"I wasn't sure about it at first, either," Rose began, "but if it can actually help Evie's anxiety, then we should give it a try."

"I just think it's crazy for our thirteen-year-old daughter to go to a prison," Noah replied.

"I know, I know, but we have to try something. Evie is so uncomfortable with this anxiety and fear. It's not fair for her to be like this."

"But we can try the new therapy Evan told you about," Noah said.

"Well, we are going to try that too. We are going to do everything we can to help our daughter."

"Dad, please," Evie pleaded. "I know this sounds crazy, but I just know that I need to do this. I have to go and see for myself that Carter is locked up. I have to talk to him. At the least, I may start to feel better and maybe I could even convince him to not want to hurt me anymore. There is so much that could come from this."

"And we will make sure that she is safe," Rose added. "She'll be safe and protected. We'll go with her."

"I can see this is important to you, Evie," Noah said. "I guess I am okay with it."

Evie then told Logan that she was going to visit his brother and he actually thought it was a good idea.

"I know if he can just get to know you better, he will like you so much, that he won't want to hurt you," Logan said. "You're so likeable."

"Well, thanks," Evie said blushing. "I hope you're right. I just hope something about this visit makes him feel differently."

One week later and Evie was on her way to visit Carter. It felt so scary entering the prison. It smelled so musty in there. It seemed damp. There was such a feeling of dread and foreboding inside. Everything was gray. The walls were all concrete and she could feel the cold seeping from them. In fact, the whole place felt cold with all the stone and metal. She hoped that she wouldn't stay long. Maybe she could accomplish her goals quickly.

The prison guard brought Carter to the table to sit across from Evie. He was bound by handcuffs. There was a window of bulletproof glass between them just like you see in the movies. Rose and Noah were sitting in the same room, behind Evie. Evie didn't know where to begin. To her surprise, Carter started.

"Well, I'm surprised to see you here," he said. "What on earth would make you want to visit me?"

"I guess it is kinda crazy," Evie said. She didn't want to tell him that she was there to see for herself that he was indeed locked up and not a threat to her anymore. "I'm not exactly sure why I'm here."

"Well, how's Logan?" Carter asked.

"He's fine," Evie answered.

"He's mad at me, isn't he? I mean, I don't blame him or anything, but I don't like him being mad at me. I miss him. He's my brother."

"I can understand that," Evie said.

"I know you didn't come to see me to talk about Logan," Carter said after a while. "So, why did you come?"

Evie paused trying to think of what to say. "I guess I do have questions."

"Well, fire away," Carter said flippantly. "I've got nothing but time."

"Do you hate me or something?" Evie asked.

"No, I don't hate you," Carter said. "I don't know you well enough to hate you."

"Then why did you try so hard to kill me?" Evie asked.

"It's complicated."

"Do you know what I am?"

"What do you mean?" Carter asked but he knew what she meant.

"I think I know why you tried to kill me but I'm not sure. If it's the reason that I think it is, then that means you know what I am."

Carter was intrigued and wanted to know more, so he confessed. "Yes, I know what you are."

"Are you one too?" Evie asked.

"Yes, I am," Carter replied.

"How did you find out about it?" Evie asked.

"I found my biological mother and she told me. At first, I didn't believe her, but she convinced me."

"Yeah, I didn't believe my parents at first either. I was like, 'guys I might love Dobby the elf, but I'm a little old to believe in these things.'" And with this, Evie let out a small, nervous laugh and Carter smiled. "But they persisted and I knew they weren't lying or kidding. How did your mom convince you?"

"First off, she's not my mom. I will never think of her as my mom."

"Oh sorry," Evie said.

"No, it's okay. But the woman who is my biological mother just persisted too and I dunno, it was just something in the way she was telling me, the way she confessed, I could tell she wasn't lying or joking, like you said. But she also said other things. Like how," then Carter lowered to a whisper, "elves can see and hear things from further away than humans. And I have experienced this, to an extreme amount actually. So that sort of convinced me too."

"Yeah, I've experienced that too. The nurse at the doctor's office couldn't believe how easily I could read the eye chart and the whole bottom row with ease."

"Yeah, me too. I had the same experience. The nurse was like, 'well, you definitely don't need glasses.'" Carter smiled again and Evie let out a nervous laugh again.

"So," Evie started, "I think I know why you wanted to kill me but I'm not completely sure. I really want to know, so I'm just going to ask. Did you want to end the elf people completely? Why would you want to end your own kind?"

"No, that's not why I did it. I don't want to end the elf people completely."

Evie was very surprised. She thought that was definitely the reason Carter had tried to kill her. "Well, that's what would happen if you killed me. I don't know if you know or not, but I'm the last chance of the elf people continuing."

"Yes, I know," Carter admitted. "My biological mother told me as much."

"Then why did you try to kill me?"

"I don't want to talk about it. Let's just say my birth mother said things that I didn't want to hear. She kicked off everything."

"But what do you mean? I really would like to know why you did all this."

Carter opened his mouth to say something but then he stopped. "I don't think I want to do this," he said. "I have to go." And with that he waved to the guard that he was ready to go.

"No, wait, what were you going to say?" Evie shouted to Carter as they hauled him off. He didn't say anything more and Evie knew right away she wanted to come back to see him again.

CHAPTER 13

SECOND VISIT & THE FORGIVENESS

It took some convincing for Evie to get her parents to agree to take her back to the prison. They didn't see the point in it. But Evie was persistent and told them how important it was to her. They committed to going again the next weekend.

This time the prison didn't seem as foreboding as it had before but it was still cold and slightly scary. Once again, the guards brought Carter out to sit across from Evie.

"Another visit? I've seen more of you than Logan," Carter said to Evie. "He's still mad at me for attacking his little girlfriend. But you probably know more about that than I do."

"Actually, Logan doesn't like talking about you," Evie replied. "But he did think it was a good idea for me to visit you. I think he wants me to see that you can be a good guy. He still cares about you."

"Well, that's good to know. I hope that one day he and I will be on good terms again. I mean, he's my only brother," Carter briefly paused. "Well, not really, but the only one I'll ever know."

"What do you mean?" Evie asked. "You have another brother?"

"I don't want to talk about it. You don't want to hear about my troubles, not after what I did to you."

"No, I do want to hear. Please, tell me about your brother."

"There's nothing to tell," Carter said. "I don't know anything about him. My biological mother told me that I have brother, that she has another son. But she wouldn't let me meet him and she didn't tell me anything about him. She doesn't want us to ever know each other. So, like I said, there's nothing to tell. I will never know him."

"That's so sad. I can't imagine having a brother and not being able to meet or know him. I would be so mad at her."

"Yeah, well, that's how special my birth mom is. She not only gave me up and never looked back but now she doesn't even want me to know my brother. Hell, she doesn't want me to know her either. I'll probably never see her again."

"Oh," Evie didn't know what to say. "Sorry your mom is like that. Or not your mom, I know you don't see her as your mom."

"You don't need to be sorry for me, especially after what I did to you. I'm starting to see that I was really mad at her, my birth mother, not you. I think I just took it all out on you. I've had *plenty* of time to think in here. I'm the one who should be sorry, obviously. I mean, I am sorry, you know."

"That's nice to hear."

"I wish I could make it up to you."

"You could. Just tell me why you tried to kill me," Evie said.

Carter sat and stared at Evie for a while. "I guess I owe it to you to tell you everything," Carter replied. "Though it still sounds pretty pathetic and not like a good enough reason to kill someone."

"It sounds like you were hurting," Evie said.

"Yeah, and I did some really stupid things. I can't believe I went so far. For some reason, I thought I would feel better if you were gone, because you were a girl, the girl that my mom wanted."

"What? What are you talking about?" Evie asked.

"Yeah, that's the whole story."

"Wait, start at the beginning," Evie said.

"You want the long version or the short version?" Carter asked.

"The long version, if you don't mind," Evie replied.

"Why would I mind? It's not like I have somewhere to be," Carter said. "Well," he continued, "I knew I was adopted. My parents had told me when I was little. It felt like I had always known. I never really gave it much thought. I mean, it didn't bother me. I had great parents, who had given me a great childhood and who really loved me. But then, I don't know, something changed. When I was around seventeen, I started really wondering about my biological parents. It was like I became obsessed with thinking about them. I was wondering who they were, where they were and especially, why had they given me up."

"Yeah, I would wonder that too," Evie said.

"I researched myself on the internet to see if I could find anything about them. I called adoption agencies and asked them for some info but no one would tell me anything. I couldn't find anything about them. I tried to stop thinking about them, but I couldn't. Like I said, it's like I was obsessed. So, I finally worked up the nerve to ask my adopted mom, my real mom, about them. I didn't want to do this because I didn't want to risk hurting her. But she was really receptive to it. My mom said my bio mom was just not ready to be a mother and that it was really hard for her to give me up. She told me she had actually heard from my mother a few times over the course of my life. That she had checked in on me and made sure I was fine. She knew who she was and where she was. My mom, though, didn't know anything about my biological dad. She had never even met him. But she assured me that my bio mom had cared for me and still did care about me."

"But that wasn't enough for you, was it?" Evie asked.

"No, it wasn't. I really wanted to meet her. I really wanted to ask her why she had given me up. So, I asked my mom if she could set up a meeting between us. She agreed to call my bio mom and ask if she would meet me. My bio mom said she would meet me but only if I came to her. That should've been my first sign, but whatever. I booked a flight and went to her. She lives up in Massachusetts. When I got there, I felt like I had made a huge mistake. She didn't seem like she wanted me there at all. It was crazy awkward. But I knew I had to do it. I went inside and we talked for a little while and it stayed awkward. I asked about my bio dad and she told me that she didn't know him anymore. She so nicely informed me that he wanted nothing to do with me or her after he found out that she was pregnant. She told me his name in case I ever wanted to look him up but he sounds like a real jerk, so I just forgot about him. Eventually, I finally got to ask what I had traveled there to ask her. I asked her why she gave me up."

"What did she say?" Evie asked.

"It was a long and uneasy answer where she was saying that she was young and not ready to be a mother. But I reminded her that she wasn't that young, she was twenty-five, and she agreed but she doubled down that she wasn't ready to be a mother and that she had no family or help because she wasn't close with her family and obviously my bio dad was no help. Then she started saying that she also wanted to focus on her career at that time. She was really rambling and it seemed like she was making it up as she went along. I wasn't buying it so I kept pressing her on what the real reason was. I think I agitated her because she kind of erupted and it burst out that she would've kept me if I had been a girl. She was disappointed that I was a boy. I was confused so she finally confessed the whole,…" Carter started whispering, "…elf thing. She told me I was an elf and how, you know, only the elf girls can have elf children. Even though I was an elf, it wasn't enough for her. She wanted to continue the elf people and if she couldn't she didn't feel like keeping me. She didn't want a boy. So, I was jealous of you because you are the elf daughter that she had wanted. She told me about you and I could see it in her face. She longed to be your mother and wanted nothing to do with me. It was all kinds of messed up."

"And that's why you tried to kill me?"

"Yeah, I know it sounds crazy and it doesn't make any sense."

"No, it does make sense," Evie replied and Carter's eyes got wide. "I understand why you did what you did. I mean, it's definitely extreme what you did, but I get it that you were hurting and you needed someone to take that out on. Your birth mom was awful to you."

"Yeah, it was after this, that she also told me she never wanted to see me again and that she never wanted me to know my biological brother. She's a real gem."

"I'm sorry for what you went through with her," Evie said.

Carter couldn't believe what Evie was saying. "How can you be so understanding? What I did to you was monstrous. I was more awful to you than my birth mother was to me."

"Well, that's true, but I still understand. Do you really mean that you are sorry?"

"Yes, I do. Especially now that you are here and saying these things. Now that I know you better, I am so sorry. I shouldn't have been trying to kill you. You had nothing to do with what my mother did to me. I am really sorry."

"Well then, I forgive you," Evie said.

"I can't believe that you forgive me. It seems so unforgiveable, what I did."

"When you get out of here, are you ever going to try to kill me again?" Evie asked.

"No, I can honestly say that I am never going to try to kill you again. I don't know, it's like I feel completely different now. I feel different about you and about elves in general. I realized I don't want our people to end. I've been thinking about it ever since you said it the other day, that if you died, there was no chance of elves continuing and I want them to continue. So, I should be trying to protect you, not trying to hurt you. I want our people to continue and that means you need to stay alive."

"That's beyond great to hear," Evie said and she could actually feel her anxiety lifting. The tightness in her chest eased and her heart felt lighter. She could finally take a nice, deep breath. Mr. Dancy had been right; this was the best treatment she could have done.

"It's nice to know another elf too," Carter continued. "I want to know another elf and since I won't know my birth mother or my brother that are elves, you may be my only chance to know another elf."

"Yeah, I don't know many other elves either, none other than my family, so it would be nice to know another elf that isn't related to me," Evie said. "I can't believe I'm saying this, but I actually think we could be friends."

"I can't believe you are saying that either. But that would be great."

"This is not what I expected to come of these visits but it's awesome. I'm so glad I visited," Evie said with a smile and Carter smiled back.

This would not be Evie's last visit to Carter. She would even visit him with Logan one day. Visiting him turned out to be a great idea. She had done it. She had accomplished the two things she set out to do. Her fear and anxiety had left her entirely. And Carter had a complete change of heart towards her. He went from wanting to kill her for some form of revenge to pledging to protect her so the elf people would continue. He would never again try to hurt the last elf daughter.